Karin Baine lives in Northern Ireland with her husband, two sons and her out-of-control notebook collection. Her mother and her grandmother's vast collection of books inspired her love of reading and her dream of becoming a Mills & Boon author. Now she can tell people she has a *proper* job! You can follow Karin on Twitter, @karinbaine1, or visit her website for the latest news—karinbaine.com.

Also by Karin Baine

French Fling to Forever
A Kiss to Change Her Life
The Doctor's Forbidden Fling
The Courage to Love Her Army Doc
Falling for the Foster Mum
Reforming the Playboy
Their Mistletoe Baby

Discover more at millsandboon.co.uk.

FROM FLING TO WEDDING RING

KARIN BAINE

MILLS & BOON

Published in Great Britain 2018
by Mills & Boon, an imprint of HarperCollins*Publishers*
1 London Bridge Street, London, SE1 9GF

ISBN: 978-0-263-93352-9

MIX
Paper from
responsible sources
FSC **FSC™ C007454**

This book is produced from independently certified FSC™ paper
to ensure responsible forest management.
For more information visit www.harpercollins.co.uk/green.

Printed and bound in Spain
by CPI, Barcelona

For Kelly and Doctor K,
who put me together again.

With thanks to Julia and Sheila
for their patience and understanding,
and to Tammy, Pat and Chellie
for helping me with the research. xx

CHAPTER ONE

Mollie focused her attention on the gun in her hand, fully aware of the implications of this moment. Tattoos were a commitment but, as she knew herself, they also had the potential to be life-changing. If not for the hours she'd spent under the needle she might never have had the confidence to leave the house at all after her accident and the numerous resulting surgeries, never mind complete her nurse training. Although she'd never fully come to terms with the scars left behind from her childhood, having the physical ones at least partially hidden gave her some comfort.

'If you need a break, just let me know.' She glanced up to check that her patient, Carole, was coping with the continued vibration of the machine against her skin, but she showed no visible signs of distress.

'I'm fine. That numbing cream you used seems to have done the trick.'

'Good. We're almost done anyway.'

As a clinical nurse specialist in the breast care centre at the Tower Hospital in London she worked closely with her patients through all stages of their treatment to ensure quality of care, from providing emotional support after that first diagnosis of breast cancer to advice and information post-treatment, but it was her role as medical tattooist that gave her most job satisfaction.

She knew how much it took for these ladies to trust her with their bodies after the trauma they'd gone through. That first time she'd had to strip off for the consultation with her tattoo artist, she'd been trembling so hard she'd imagined the only art possible was squiggly lines and splodges, but the sympathetic, caring nature of the woman she'd soon come to see regularly had put her at ease. She wanted to recreate that feeling of safety and privacy for everyone who came through the doors of her clinic as well as leaving them with a sense of pride in their appearance.

Some women who'd decided their bodies had been through enough after chemotherapy and surgery opted for the tattoo only rather than go through a breast reconstruction after a mastectomy, while others decided to make use of the prostheses and stick-on artificial nipples available. It was a personal choice for each individual patient, one not arrived at easily, and it was her job to inform them of the options available. This final decision was the road back for these women reclaiming their bodies and femininity from cancer.

She'd been there to support Carole during her difficult decision to have her breast reconstruction at the same time as her mastectomy six months ago and for her sake wanted to get the all-important shading right with the medical grade micro-pigment to create the 3D effect of the areola around the reconstructed nipple to complete the transformation. Hopefully this would be the last surgical step for her.

'It looks so real. I can't thank you enough.' Carole's eyes were shining with tears of gratitude as Mollie cleaned the wound one last time and switched off the tattoo machine.

She gave a cough to clear the ball of emotion wedged in her throat as she removed the sheet partially covering Carole's upper half. It was impossible to accompany people on this journey without becoming emotionally attached.

'You can take a good look in the mirror to make sure you're happy before I put the dressing on.'

Though Mollie had never suffered from cancer herself, being able to look in the mirror without recoiling had been an important part of her recovery process and she was privileged to be in a position to do the same for other people. Even if she wasn't convinced other people didn't look at her scars without judgement, and still kept them covered as much as possible.

'You've done an incredible job… I don't know why I'm crying…' Carole laughed through her tears as she eased her clothes on. She'd been stoic throughout the counselling sessions during her treatment and it was only human for those emotions she'd been holding back during her battle to come flooding out now it was coming to an end.

'It's a natural reaction, Carole. You've been through a lot. Now, do you have anyone you can talk to if you need to until I see you again?' Although they'd discussed the course available to her with a clinical psychologist to help rebuild her confidence, it wouldn't be right to just send her home now with no immediate emotional support.

'My husband's been great, as you know, but my sister has invited me to stay with her for a few days in the country so I think I might take her up on the offer.'

'Good idea. The break will do you good and we're

only on the end of the phone if you need to talk to any of us. Leave that dressing on for forty-eight hours and try not to get it wet for the next ten days or so. As we discussed, we'll send you out an appointment in about six weeks for a top-up to prevent any fading, but if you experience any swelling or a rise in temperature between now and then, please speak to your doctor in case any infection should develop.' All aftercare instructions were in the leaflets Mollie passed on but they were worth repeating when there was always that small risk of complication occurring.

'I will. Thank you. I'm quite looking forward to some peace and quiet. Not to mention a bit of TLC. Even at sixty-three, I'm still considered the baby of the family.' Carole rolled her eyes as she folded the information sheets for perusal later.

Although only the eldest by two minutes and sixteen seconds, Mollie understood that need to protect her little sister, too. Not that she'd been given much choice, with Talia having inherited their mother's laissez-faire attitude to responsibility. Someone had had to step up and be the adult after their father abandoned them and, since Mollie was the one to blame for him leaving, that someone had been her.

The stress of her injuries and multiple surgeries had taken its toll on her parents financially and driven her volatile father to take out his frustrations on her mother and sister. If she'd done as she was told and kept away from that old building at the end of the road she would never have slipped and been ripped to shreds falling through that glass window and shattered the family. Trying to emulate Talia's daredevil defiance had been an immature attempt to grab some of the local boys' attention away from her pretty sister and had ultimately ruined her life and everyone else's.

It was the guilt of being the catalyst for that escalating violence and eventual abandonment that had kept her at home looking after their broken-hearted mother and left her indebted to her sister. They'd paid the price for her actions and carried as many scars as she did.

There was a hard, sharp rap on the door—the kind she associated with medical emergencies or anxious family members impatient for news—which dragged her out of those dark memories and back into the present.

'Come in,' she shouted, half expecting to see a worried Mr Rogers keen for news on his wife's progress. He attended all Carole's appointments with her, even if he didn't sit in on counselling sessions, and they always left holding hands. It was the kind of sweet relationship she wished her mother had found after their father had left, instead of the string of disastrous affairs she'd fallen into over the years, her confidence knocked into submission long ago. Perhaps if she had found that support in a partner life would've turned out so very differently for them both where Mollie wouldn't have felt indebted to fill the role. She might even have harboured some small desire to find love herself if she'd seen evidence it existed. As it was she'd be happy simply to have some space of her own.

The door opened and there was a brief flutter of panic in her chest that it might have been one of *her* family members come to seek her counsel. It wouldn't be the first time her mother had rolled up here, tear-stained and hungover after a row with her latest boyfriend, expecting her daughter to be sympathetic. Now that Talia was working in the nearby emergency department, there was every possibility she could turn up at any given moment, too.

Her relief when a beaming male figure strode into the room was short-lived. It wasn't the kindly Mr Rogers, who made her hidden romantic sigh, but Ben Sheridan, Consultant Plastic and Reconstructive Surgeon at the clinic, who had the uncanny ability to make every nerve in her body tighten until she was sure one day they would all snap and leave her lying on the floor before him like a puppet with its strings cut.

'Sorry to interrupt, Nurse Forrester, I just wanted to check up on my favourite patient.' He breezed past her in a waft of spicy aftershave towards the now positively girlish Carole, who was blushing and waving away the flattery.

'Sure. Don't mind me.' Mollie dropped the used cotton balls and antiseptic wipes into the bin, letting the lid slam shut in a pique of temper.

Her job in maintaining the link between patients and the health-care professionals meant their paths crossed regularly at the multidisciplinary team meetings where they discussed cases and recommendations for treatment. Those who'd witnessed him transform patients' lives beneath his scalpel had declared him as a 'brilliant young surgeon.' It was a shame that with that brilliance also came a self-righteousness that he thought gave him a right to bawl her out when they'd had a difference of opinion over a patient's treatment. She'd known the patient's desire to keep as much of her own breast tissue as possible but Ben had pulled rank, insisting there was no option but to perform a complete mastectomy to remove all traces and possibility of cancer.

Whether he'd been correct in his judgement or not, it hadn't given him the right to yell at her the way he had that morning. He obviously thought that being at the top of his field meant that no one else could question his decisions, but she was every bit as confident in her role as he was in his. She would never question that he was the expert when it came to reconstructive surgery but she knew the patients on a personal level and she reckoned that counted just as much when deciding on the best course of treatment to suit an individual's needs.

Mollie didn't often hold grudges but when it came to questioning her professional abilities she was willing to make an exception for Ben Sheridan.

When he came here, 'checking up,' her paranoia kicked in that he suspected there was a danger she might undo his good work during this final stage and that their conflict might turn out to be more than a one-off.

'I'm fine, Doctor. Mollie here has been wonderful.' Carole's praise was a welcome affirmation to him that she knew what she was doing.

'Good to know I left you in such capable hands.' Ben nodded an acknowledgement Mollie was sure was nothing more than professional courtesy yet heat prickled her skin as that cobalt stare lit upon her. Those ever-watchful blue eyes contrasting against the near black, neatly groomed hair and dark beard made him an imposing figure. Not to mention a handsome one. Two factors that had an unsettling effect on her pulse.

'It might seem like a lot to ask now, but the best thing you can do for yourself is to keep looking in the mirror and learn to accept these changes are part of everything which makes you the beautiful person you are.' She kept her back to Ben while she gave Carole the pep talk, conscious he was here watching and listening.

There were so many reasons she felt uncomfortable around him, but it was the attraction she felt towards

him despite their obvious personality clash that un-
nerved her most. He had a reputation among the nursing
staff as much for his antics outside the operating theatre
as inside it. It had been noted that he'd attended every
hospital event in recent times with a different woman
on his arm and appeared to lead a very interesting and
varied personal life. Unlike her own.

She'd learned at an early age men usually preferred
trophy girlfriends to scarred, damaged women with too
many personal issues to stuff into a designer clutch bag,
and had steered clear since.

Work, home, eat, sleep, repeat—that was her routine
and she was happy as long as she was allowed to get
on with it in peace.

'Well, we're all finished now...'

There's no need for you to stick around, Ben...

Carole's phone beeped with an incoming text message and Mollie bent down to retrieve her handbag from
the floor to save her stretching for it.

'I'll get it—'

'Let me—'

Unfortunately Ben reached for it at the same time
and accidentally grabbed her hand instead of the bag.
The unexpected jolt from the touch of his skin on hers
almost knocked her onto her backside.

She scrambled to her feet and let him do the hon-
ours, since the room suddenly seemed much too small
to accommodate his sizeable frame along with hers and
Carole's.

'That's my husband. I should go and put him out of
his misery and tell him we're all finished.'

'Great. I'll say a quick hello while I'm here.' Ben—
seemingly eager to put some space between them, too—

escorted Carole out of the door and let Mollie breathe a little easier.

'I'll see you in a few weeks' time, Carole.' The moment Mollie waved them off and shut the door, she collapsed back into her chair. A quick glance at her watch confirmed she had time before her next appointment to grab a break and regain her composure.

It was ridiculous that she should get so flustered when she knew she was damn good at her job, but he had that knack of upsetting the status quo around here. No matter how busy they were at the clinic, there was always that ripple of excitement accompanying a visit from Mr Sheridan, which was not reserved solely for her. Staff and patients alike lit up whenever he was around.

Some days it was like an episode of one of those awful reality shows where women competed against each other in the hope of winning the coveted prize of a date with the handsome star attraction. Thank goodness she had no inclination towards any man who treated women as nothing more than accessories. Her mother had paraded enough of those through her life to leave her immune. There seemed little point in adding a man to the list of people she had to worry about or who could cause her more pain, and no reason this man in particular should make her rethink that now.

There was another rap on the door but this time it opened before she'd even had time to reply.

'I wanted to thank you—' Just when she thought it was safe to relax, Ben popped his head around the door again and every fibre of her being tightened back to breaking point.

'Er...no problem. It is my job, after all.'

It really didn't require his personal attention. She

did this every day of the week without waiting for his approval like an eager pupil expecting a gold star from her teacher for completing her homework.

Instead of ending the conversation and closing the door, he seemed to take it as an invitation to step back inside the room.

'I don't mean the tattoo. I've seen your work and have no doubt you've done a sterling job as usual. I'm talking about putting yourself forward for the dance competition. I know we haven't always seen eye to eye and I appreciate—'

Mollie stopped tidying away her supplies as her world seemed to come screeching to a halt. 'Pardon me?'

'The fundraiser, for The Men's Shed project? Your name was on the list of volunteers...' The deep frown ploughed through his forehead gave no indication that this was a joke and yet Mollie had an uncontrollable urge to laugh. As if prancing about in sequins before an audience was anything she'd participate in willingly. The very idea was the stuff of nightmares for someone who was self-conscious enough about the way she looked. Never mind that she couldn't actually dance, the last thing she needed was people judging her with a score card and a sharp tongue.

'I think someone's pulling your leg. Or mine.' This was clearly someone's idea of a joke and one made at her expense. Her carefully applied make-up and flair for vintage fashion might make it seem as though she were bursting with confidence but that was the trick. That hard shell had been carefully created to protect the fragile ego inside. A dance contest was actually so far out of her comfort zone she'd need a search and rescue team to find her way back from the spotlight.

'Oh. You'd think people would know better than to mess around with a charity.' Or to waste the time of a very busy surgeon whose frown had now deepened into more of a scowl and did nothing to stop the current shivers hurdling over her spine.

'Sorry. Is this your project?' Even though she was gasping for a cup of tea to settle her nerves, it seemed churlish to chivvy him out of her room now when he'd been sent on a wild goose chase on her behalf.

'I volunteered to help raise funds but the dancing part was not my idea.' He winced as though he'd been held at gunpoint and personally forced into tight hot-pink fabric. Now that was something she was sure a lot of people would pay good money to see, her included.

'And what is this "Shed" exactly?'

'It's a community hub where elderly men can socialise and keep active. We need funds to renovate the place and I'd hate to see it fold when it's already doing so much to help those who might otherwise be isolated from society.' His ownership of the project and the financial problems it was having softened the hard edge of the man she'd encountered at that fraught staff meeting. It spoke volumes about his personal involvement and commitment, and somehow made him seem more human, more likeable than some of the other bigwigs who often paid little more than lip service to the charities they allegedly supported. Half the time Mollie wondered if it wasn't more about raising their personal profiles and scoring extra points on their CVs than being charitable.

'You *can* put my name down for a couple of tickets for the show. I'd be happy to make a donation.' No matter how deserving a cause, Mollie would much rather watch than participate. She shouldn't have much trouble convincing Talia to go as her plus one when she was always going on about her getting out and having some fun these days.

That was easier said than done when you weren't the blonde-haired, blue-eyed twin with the perfect body and no discernible responsibilities.

'I'll be sure to get it in writing this time.' His self-deprecating smile was unexpected, as was the warm glow that seemed to start in Mollie's toes and spread steadily throughout the rest of her body.

A lot of the highly skilled, in-demand surgical professionals she'd come across in the workplace had a superiority complex the same size as their impressive list of qualifications and would have ranted and raved about wasting their time. She'd certainly seen evidence of his temper, which would be justified on an occasion where he'd been inconvenienced by some unknown prankster. His understanding that she was an unwitting participant in this made her feel a tad ashamed of her conjecture on his character formed from one emotionally charged disagreement, when that judgement was exactly what terrified her most. It was a shock to discover her greatest fear turned out to be her own biggest personal flaw.

She hated people making assumptions about her, that her tattoos or her clothes somehow defined her as weird, or, worse, that her dedication to her job and her family marked her as a loner. Yet she knew she had a habit of jumping to conclusions about people based on first impressions. It was a defence mechanism that she'd developed over the years to protect herself from anyone else who showed a proclivity towards violence to avoid any more nasty surprises further down the line.

A history including an abusive father, a supposed

loving boyfriend who rejected her after seeing her scars for the first time and a series of partners who eventually lost patience when she couldn't bring herself to sleep with them, made it difficult to trust anything other than her own instincts.

On this occasion she might be proven wrong, but although discovering the possibility Ben was a nicer guy than she'd imagined would explain his popularity with women who weren't her, it didn't make her any more willing to participate in this spectacle. She'd conned herself once into believing she should put herself at risk simply to gain the approval of a good-looking boy and paid the price. It would take more than a playboy surgeon to change her mind after all these years.

'Well, good luck with it.' She gave him his cue to leave so they could both get back to work and forget this little incident ever happened.

'Right. Sorry for wasting your time.' Ben backed out of the room and only just managed to refrain from swearing in the busy corridor. That hadn't gone as smoothly as he'd planned. Although he'd been glad to see Carole in good spirits after her surgery his visit to the clinic had left him with more problems than he'd arrived with. Now he was one dancer short for his fundraising event and, in particular, the one he'd seen himself paired with—The Ice Queen. Someone's idea of a joke was going to cost him time tracking down a new volunteer, not to mention peace of mind.

When he'd seen Nurse Forrester's name on the list for the forthcoming competition he'd thought she'd finally forgiven him for that outburst the other week. Things had been a bit strained between them since he'd lost his temper and, though he was embarrassed about it, he couldn't explain his mood without coming across as unprofessional. It didn't matter how little sleep he'd had or how rough his night had been at home, he should never have brought it into the workplace with him. His private life was no one else's business.

Having her back onside would also have produced the ideal solution to his search for a partner. Although he'd never heard anything but praise from their shared patient list, never witnessed anything other than professionalism when they'd worked together, he'd heard the locker room talk about The Ice Queen from porters to surgeons who'd tried to secure a date with the pretty brunette and been shot down mid-chat-up. For those delicate male egos who weren't used to being turned down, they'd somehow managed to turn her lack of interest in them into a character assassination and something she should be castigated for rather than a comment on their own arrogance or shortcomings.

Her involvement would've curtailed any further rumours about his alleged philandering or romantic ideas towards, or from, a woman whose smile faltered any time he paid a visit to shared patients. He'd even felt her flinch today when they'd happened to come into close proximity and almost sympathised with those she'd shown her obvious contempt for in the past. She didn't know him any more than he knew her and, though it would be easy to believe those rumours that she hated men, he knew not to take the gossipmongers at face value.

Despite the lack of chemistry required for a dance partnership, this would've provided him with an uncomplicated route to the finish line of this fundraising born out of necessity rather than a desire to strut his stuff on a public dance floor.

His mobile phone vibrated in his pocket and he made a quick dash for the exit to answer it to avoid disturbing the clinic any further. Thankfully the noise of running car engines and nearby construction drowned out the profanity that did slip out of his mouth this time when he saw who it was calling, because it meant there was undoubtedly another catastrophe happening at home.

'Is everything all right, Grandad?'

'Someone's stolen my glasses. I think it's that woman who comes here every morning.' Unfortunately, as had become the custom, the phone call was not to check in with Ben but to launch another accusation about the carer who came in to make his grandfather's meals when he was at work. He was sure she'd no more stolen his glasses today than she had sewn up the cuffs of his cardigan when he couldn't get it on last week. The truth was Hugh Sheridan was getting old, and struggling to live with this cruel illness more every day, even if neither of them were ready to acknowledge it yet.

He'd lost so much weight due to the meals he'd forgotten to eat, or the out-of-date food he'd sickened himself with, it had become apparent he could no longer look after himself, but it had been a job for Ben to get him to move into his apartment where he could keep an eye on him. In the end he'd had to convince him *he* wanted the company, not that he believed his grandfather was a danger to himself. The move had been the final nail in the coffin of his relationship with Penny and everyone else who was afraid they might be expected to play nursemaid to a septuagenarian.

Even his own parents had abandoned them, because it suited them and their jet-set lifestyle to let Ben assume the role of carer. Not that he'd expect anything more from people who'd given up on their son so easily. They would've been as happy to pack his grandfather off to an old people's home as they had been to send their wayward child away without a second thought about why he'd fallen in with a bad crowd. It was easier on their consciences to absolve themselves of any responsibility other than a visit on special occasions or the odd phone call than to examine their own failure as parents.

Underage drinking, graffiti...vandalism had all seemed like harmless fun in the company of the wrong crowd, as had defying his parents, until he'd pushed them to breaking point. He saw now his actions had shown a desperate need for someone to provide boundaries and guide him in the right direction when he'd been too easily seduced by the idea of rebellion. An unheeded cry for help. It had taken the faith and courage of his grandparents to see that there was someone worth saving beneath that troublesome exterior when not even his parents had been convinced.

Although he maintained some semblance of a relationship with them, it was always at the back of his mind that they might still be waiting for his illustrious career to come crashing down around him in another fit of self-destruction. Despite turning his life around, there was a distance between them that suggested they were afraid to become too proud of him in case the day ever came when they'd get the chance to say, 'See, we knew he was a wrong 'un.'

Regardless of his career success, they justified their absence from his life by pointing out he didn't have any children for them to come back for. As if they would have been any more attentive to grandchildren than to their only son. Deserting him when he was in need of their help now as an adult didn't hurt any less than it had as a teenager, it merely reinforced the belief he wasn't important enough in their lives to deserve time out of their busy schedule. It had been just him and his grandfather for some time now.

They were the only tie he still had to that old life and perhaps that was the reason he kept them at arm's length, too—they were a reminder of times that didn't make him particularly proud of himself and were a far cry, hopefully, from the respected man he'd become. He didn't blame his parents for becoming exasperated with their son's behaviour, he knew now how stressed they must have been, but neither did he credit them with any part of his success since. That was reserved for the man who was currently wandering his apartment in search of more misplaced personal items.

'That's Amy, remember? She comes to help out when I'm at work.' It had been getting harder by the day to juggle his time here at the hospital and at home and she'd been a godsend as far as Ben was concerned. At least now he could go into Theatre with the knowledge there'd be someone to check that the apartment hadn't burned down in his absence. His grandfather was becoming more and more forgetful, as well as belligerent, as the cruel spectre of dementia hovered around him.

There was an unintelligible grumble on the other end of the line suggesting he didn't entirely trust his grandson's version of events. As though there were collusion going on between the two of them to gradually steal his belongings and sanity piece by painful piece.

'Have you checked the bathroom window sill? Sometimes you leave them there.' Or actually *in* the bath, where he'd found the TV remote control last night.

'I didn't leave them anywhere. *She's* taken them.' His grandfather adamantly continued his protest without considering any alternative reason for the disappearing spectacles. It was this continual forgetfulness and paranoia that was hard to get used to but, thankfully, the good days still outnumbered the bad. The man who'd practically raised him was still more *present* than this somewhat more difficult version, or his parents. With Amy's added help, they were able to function as normally as could be expected.

However, it didn't take a medical professional to understand this wasn't an illness that would be miraculously cured. There was little even a skilled surgeon could do to prevent dementia taking hold of a beloved family member except help him cling onto his independence and dignity as long as possible. And perhaps help him find any misplaced personal possessions. The least he could do for the man who'd given him a second chance when no one else would.

'Do you want me to come back and help you find them?' He checked his watch. Now that he wouldn't be discussing dance steps or music choices he had a little time before his next appointment. Although that time could've been better utilised answering the hundreds of emails he received every day, half an hour retracing his grandfather's steps around the apartment would probably put both of their minds at rest for the remainder of the afternoon. Even if it was a stark contrast to the one he'd imagined.

'No. You're busy, son. There are a lot of people depending on you... I don't know who she thinks she is just letting herself in here when she feels like it...' Sometimes it was hard to tell if the moment of lucidity had passed or he was just having a bad-tempered rant because his independence was being compromised.

'I'm not due back in surgery for a while. I can spare ten minutes to see if I can help you find these glasses.'

He'd make a call to Amy, too, to apologise for any extra rudeness she might have encountered on this morning's visit, although her previous experience of caring for elderly patients seemed to make her quite impervious to her charge's changeable moods.

'Why would I need help finding my glasses? Sure, they're right here in my pocket where they always are.' The gruff denial that he needed help ended the call abruptly and left Ben standing outside the hospital contemplating whether or not to go back inside.

It was these divided loyalties that tested every area of his life, as well as those around him. He'd already had one relationship disintegrate under the pressure of his responsibilities as a carer and, though he'd had a few dalliances since, his love life wasn't any more of a priority than a dependent elderly relative was for those he'd dated. The reputation he'd acquired of being a ladies' man wasn't surprising since he still enjoyed female company, but unjustified, when any notion of a relationship barely lasted beyond dessert.

He fished his car keys from his pocket and strode towards the staff car park. It wouldn't do any harm to call back home for five minutes and make sure all was well. His hunt for a partner came second to the needs of his grandfather. As did everything else in his personal life.

Mollie Forrester would've been the perfect answer to getting him out of the dance competition pickle he'd found himself in and he wondered if there wasn't still time to talk her around.

After all, he wasn't one to walk away at the first sign of trouble.

CHAPTER TWO

'So, WHAT ARE your plans for the weekend?' Talia queried once she'd swallowed the large bite she'd taken of her chicken salad sandwich. Her appetite certainly seemed to have improved since her return and Mollie was pleased in that motherly way that she was eating properly instead of skipping meals as she'd often been prone to doing before heading out for an evening of partying. These days she was more likely to be found at night propping up the other end of the sofa from her sister watching TV.

'Um…laundry, decluttering my wardrobe, washing my hair…' She'd neglected to mention Ben Sheridan's strange visit or they would've spent the rest of their short meal break together arguing about how she shouldn't have turned him down and how she would live the rest of her days as a dried-up old spinster full of regret.

'Sounds like a riot.' Talia rolled her eyes, apparently unimpressed by the proposed itinerary.

'That doesn't mean you have to stay in, too. There's nothing stopping you from going clubbing or whatever it usually is you do in your time off.' Mollie had never been one for the party circuit where copious amounts of alcohol and rash decisions often went hand in hand. Not since she'd suffered the ugly fallout of her previous poor judgement. Talia had done enough *living* for the both of them, even if the pace of her partying seemed to have slowed in the weeks since she'd come home from her travels.

Although it was Mollie who'd encouraged her to spread her beautiful butterfly wings when the job opportunity abroad had arisen at the end of their nurse training, she hadn't realised the lonely life she'd condemned herself to in the process. She'd wanted to give Talia a new start, a new life away from the cruel childhood memories of home, but it had only been the start of a series of posts that had taken her all around the world and further and further away.

At least, until recently. Whatever had happened during those years of 'finding herself' and working the wanderlust out of her system, she was now pushing Mollie to explore her independence a little more, too. If Talia truly had returned as the more contented adult she claimed to be, not only did it mean having someone to share the problems at home, it would alleviate some of Mollie's guilt from the past and offered her a slice of freedom she hoped hadn't come too late to enjoy.

'I've had my fun, Moll, and my time away has made me realise how unfair it was to leave you holding the fort back here with Mum all this time. I haven't been much of a sister to you.' It was an unexpected acknowledgement of her sometimes selfish behaviour, but Mollie didn't hold a grudge when they hadn't had the best role models in life from whom to take their cue.

'I wouldn't change you for the world.' She gave her sister a friendly nudge with her shoulder.

There had been times, when she was consoling her mother after her latest heartbreak or trying to untangle her messy finances, when she'd wished her sister had been around to share the burden, but she also admired Talia's free spirit. At least one of them had had the courage to put herself out there.

'Well, it's your turn now. I'm here to help out a bit more and give you the freedom you deserve. Which reminds me, weren't you supposed to be going flat hunting at some point?'

'I'm looking into it.'

'Good. Mum and I have relied on you too much over the years to be the sensible one. You need to get out and have a bit of fun.' Talia flicked the crumbs off her lap onto the grass for the sparrows hopping nearby.

'I don't know what's brought on this sudden interest in my personal life but there's no need to worry. I really have enough to keep me occupied in between shifts.'

'Oh, yes, laundry and decluttering wardrobes are so much fun.' There was no mistaking the sarcasm coming from a woman who'd probably done neither in her lifetime.

'You forgot the hair washing—' The truth was it suited Mollie to be so caught up in the mess at home when it always provided an excuse for her not to go out after work for drinks with her colleagues or those awful blind dates people kept trying to set her up on. There was no pressure to look or act a certain way when she was in her comfort zone, behind closed doors.

'Well, I've organised something much more exciting to fill your time.' There was something ominous in Talia's tone as she tidied away the remnants of their al fresco lunch on the strip of greenery surrounding the hospital intended to give the illusion they were somewhere more tranquil than central London.

'What have you done?' Since her sister's idea of fun usually involved high-octane, pulse-racing pursuits, she automatically went on meerkat alert, watching and listening for danger coming so she could take appropriate action.

'I put your name down for that dance competition they're doing. I thought a bit of excitement would do you good.'

The casual manner in which Talia tossed the information to her gave no credence to the chaos unleashed with those few words. Mollie could almost hear the ping as her nerves finally gave way with the implications of her sister's actions. That image of a scowling surgeon once he'd realised his valuable time had been wasted came to mind and sent shudders across her skin. She might've had the upper hand then, when she was the innocent party, but his patience might not accommodate a meddling sister. The custom in this sort of situation had always been for Mollie to take the flak anyone directed at her sibling. Such was the burden of guilt.

'Why would you do that?' Her voice reached soprano level as she fought to understand what would make her sister carry out such an act of stupidity when she'd only just secured her own position in the hospital.

'Because I knew you wouldn't,' Talia answered with a huff, as if that excused everything. Perhaps she hadn't done as much growing up as hoped.

'That's because it's the last thing on this earth I would ever want to do.' Her temperature was steadily rising along with her heart rate.

'Gowns and glitz…what's not to love?'

'Er…a load of people staring at me.' The very idea of shuffling around the dance floor in one of those flouncy ballroom dresses was already bringing her out in a cold sweat and that was before they even acknowledged the fact that she couldn't dance.

Talia had never really understood Mollie's anxiety about her appearance, probably because she'd never confided in her about how much it had affected her. It had been easier to simply accept the 'boring twin' tag than attempt a mature conversation on a painful subject.

'It's only a bit of fun and, you know, there are all those sexy young doctors for you to tango with...' Male attention had always been Talia's solution to any worries and Mollie had never corrected her when she assumed the one disastrous serious relationship she'd forayed into was the reason she preferred the single life. While it had contributed, her ex's horrified reaction to seeing her naked body, pretattoos, had plunged the dagger into what little left there had been of her self-confidence. There was no way she was tangoing with anyone, fully clothed or otherwise.

'If you're so keen, why didn't you volunteer?' There hadn't been any sign of a significant other, nor had Talia shown any interest in venturing into the dating pool herself lately, which was so unlike her. Mollie was sure there'd been some sort of heartbreak behind her sudden desire to come home, not that she'd admitted it so far except to say things hadn't worked out the way she'd planned.

'I'm still a newbie around here. I doubt I'd bring in the money a well-established, well-respected specialist nurse could raise for a good cause.'

Flattery didn't work with Mollie—compliments of any kind always made her suspicious when she was so aware of her every flaw—but she could see Talia's intentions had been honourable. If there was one thing Mollie would always prioritise over her own comfort it was her sister's welfare. She *was* still a newbie and Mollie didn't want her new start jeopardised because she'd unintentionally ticked off senior staff. It could be easily rectified and they both knew it was only a matter of time before she caved and did whatever her sister wanted anyway. Her part in this well-rehearsed dance was to at least make a half-hearted protest so she didn't seem like a complete pushover.

'Do not *ever* volunteer me for anything else again.' She knew Talia was only trying to help in her own way and didn't want to discourage her from future endeavours—as long as it didn't include putting her forward for things without her express consent first—but it was going to take all the courage she could summon to face Ben Sheridan and tell him there'd been a mix-up and she would be taking part after all.

That conversation wasn't the only issue liable to keep her awake at night. Dancing would leave her exposed in ways she'd avoided for over a decade.

Tracking down a surgeon was no mean feat in a busy hospital. Mollie couldn't even be sure he was here when he was in such high demand around the country. She'd refrained from having someone page him, doubting she could justify this as an emergency even if it was to her. She wouldn't be able to relax until she'd sorted this mess out. Although, confirming her participation in the competition was merely going to create another problem for her to obsess over and direct her anxiety down another path.

By the end of her shift and numerous phone calls to the relevant departments it eventually became apparent that he was no longer in the building.

'Try The Shed,' was the general advice forwarded by those staff members who took an interest in his private life.

She could've waited until the next day to ask him to reinstate her place in the competition but when further enquiries, and a quick internet search, revealed The Shed was only two stops away on the Tube she decided to rip the sticking plaster off as quick as possible.

Just because she'd taken time to change and refresh her make-up before leaving work it didn't mean she was making an extra effort for a certain surgeon. She wanted the protection of her most effective armour before going into battle.

Her vintage style was an acquired taste for some, but it had never been intended for anyone else's benefit other than her own. That fifties' retro look had seemed so glamorous to a young girl who'd struggled to accept her disfigured body and, after the accident, she'd adopted it in an attempt to project that confident image she so envied. She was grateful her face hadn't been left permanently scarred in the accident and she liked to make the most of her best asset to take the focus off those areas she constantly worried about. The moment she painted on that bright red lipstick and winged black eyeliner she at least looked as though she were ready to tackle the outside world even if she was quaking on the inside.

It was only when she turned the corner towards the slightly run-down row of commercial buildings that she wobbled ever so slightly in her navy-and-white polka-dot platform shoes. Far from the glorified outhouse she'd pictured in her mind, 'The Shed' was housed on glass-fronted shop premises with the man she'd come to see visible through the window, or at least the bottom half of him encased in paint-splattered tight denim standing at the top of a ladder. The sight made her question if she was doing the right thing by encroaching on his personal time when he was clearly no longer in professional doctor mode. When she stopped to think about it she wouldn't have appreciated him turning up at her house unannounced.

He began to descend the ladder and her chance for escape vanished as he spotted her through the window and waved her in with one hand while balancing a paint tray and paintbrush in the other.

'Mollie!' The sounds of hammering and drilling ceased as he announced her entrance to the room full of volunteers.

'Hi,' she mumbled, trying to block out all the eyes trained on their exchange.

The sudden turnaround on her decision to take part might cause him even more inconvenience and she'd no idea how this news was going to be received. With any luck he'd already picked up another partner since they'd last spoken, all this worry was for nothing and they could go back to being members of staff whose paths occasionally crossed during the course of their mutual patients' treatment.

'What brings you here? The sudden urge to brush up on your carpentry skills or add your name to our list of volunteers?' The friendly welcome was a far cry from the prickly atmosphere that had developed between them at work and took Mollie by surprise. If he was disturbed by her sudden appearance he hid it very well as he guided her away from the centre of attention towards the back of the room, leaving everyone else to go back to their woodwork and chat.

'Er…maybe next time. Although I'm not entirely sure what I could do to help.' Seeing him sacrifice what little time he probably had free on his busy schedule guilt-tripped her into suggesting she might be talked into a second visit. One that would see her rolling up her sleeves and getting dirty, no less.

'Every little helps. I can't say my own skills go beyond touching up the paintwork every now and again but I try. As you can see.' He gave an apologetic nod towards his emulsion-covered attire, which drew Mollie's attention to the faded grey T-shirt stretched tight across his broad chest. It left much less to the imagination than the loose cotton shirt he'd been wearing earlier. Probably for health and safety reasons when that small patch of smooth skin showing through the sizeable rip in the shoulder seam was so distracting.

She forced herself to maintain eye contact. 'It looks great. Fresh.'

'We're expecting the dance competition to bring us a lot of interest in the local press so we're trying to spruce the place up. We want any potential donors or sponsors to see the potential in keeping this going for the community.'

She could see that they were all working hard to make a good impression on those who held The Shed's sustainability in the folds of their wallets, as there was as much cleaning going on around here as there was woodworking. That urge to offer her help became too great for her conscience to ignore.

'Perhaps I could come back some time and paint a mural on the wall to brighten things up a bit?' She was already thinking of how she could add trailing vines and other elements inspired by nature to give the workspace more colour and character and make it seem more homely and less clinical. If he was willing to offer an olive branch there was no reason she couldn't do the same.

'That would be amazing! Thank you.'

'The reason I actually came here—' She tried to steer them back towards the purpose of the visit before she ingratiated herself any further into this little group.

'Would you like a tour?' In his delight at having secured another member into their army, he apparently didn't seem to care about why she was here and only that the enchantment of watching their endeavours would keep her here.

Before she could decline he'd rested his hand in the small of her back and was gently manoeuvring her towards the source of the noise hammering away in the background. Even though he was touching a part of her body that didn't usually cause her any discomfort—untarnished by jagged reminders of the accident—that slight contact made her skin burn with the same self-awareness. It was a long time since anyone had laid a hand on her but she was going to have to get used to it if she was expecting to take up ballroom dancing.

'This is Tom, our man in charge.'

He seemed oblivious to the tingling sensation he was causing to ripple across her skin as he introduced her to the older man in the navy coveralls and safety glasses. In the end she had to take a step away to break the contact under the guise of saying hello to Tom, who was planing long lengths of wood at the back of the shop.

Ben continued with the tour to show her the fruits of their labour lining the walls. 'The men start off with small projects, such as planters and bird boxes, which they go on to sell and raise funds for more materials, but the experts like Tom here have progressed to things like dog kennels and tables. We even recycle the offcuts of timber and bag them up for firewood to help with the costs. We don't like to waste anything here.'

Including time, Mollie suspected, which brought her

back to the reason she'd spared some of hers to come here tonight. 'I'm very impressed with the whole set-up but I actually came here to tell you I've had a change of heart over the dance competition. I am going to take part after all. If it's not too late to re-register my interest?'

She didn't enjoy portraying herself as indecisive or as flaky as some of her family members when she'd always prided herself on being the reliable one. This turnaround only hours after denying all knowledge of her addition to the list of competitors could seem as though she was just being contrary this afternoon because he'd interrupted her clinic.

He raised an eyebrow but thankfully didn't question the change of heart. 'Not at all. It saves me having to strong-arm a reluctant replacement to make up the numbers.'

Somehow she doubted he'd have trouble trying to persuade anybody to do anything. If she'd waited until tomorrow to tell him there would probably have been a queue of women waiting to take her place in his good books. It was the sound of her sister's voice in her head telling her she needed to get a life of her own that stopped her from backing out again. She might've made the mistake in thinking he cared about who took part in this competition but Talia was probably right—it would do her good to do something out of her usual routine.

'So, is there an information day or something where the couples will be announced?' Now she'd committed to taking part she was keen to know the finer details, and her mother had forced her to watch enough of those dancing shows to know it was a big deal to find out who you were paired with. Okay, she doubted there were any celebrities in the mix, but she was sure they'd create something of a buzz to kick-start the interest in tickets for the event. Although she wasn't eager to get up close and personal with her colleagues any time soon, it might put her mind at rest if the other half of her team had some sort of dance experience. She didn't want to be the joke act of the competition, literally being dragged around the floor with all the grace of a baby elephant.

'We did the launch this afternoon. That's why I came looking for you…' He shrugged an apology but Mollie was happy to have dodged whatever spectacle had taken place. She wouldn't be so lucky next time.

'Sorry. I really didn't mean to mess you around.' It was Talia who should be taking the heat for this and standing here hanging her head in shame, not her. She might have covered for her sister's screw-ups when they were kids but, as she was professing to be a grown-up now, this was the last time.

'No harm done.' Either the paint fumes had got to him or he was genuinely a much more relaxed man outside work, because he didn't appear fazed at all by the inconvenience.

Mollie, on the other hand, had spent every second since clocking off having this conversation in her head, imagining being forced to make a grovelling apology while his temper exploded again like Bonfire Night fireworks. Now she was wondering if she should have worried at all and simply left things alone.

'If you could give me the details of whoever my partner is, I'll be on my way.' A name or a number would be sufficient so she could go and collapse into a puddle of nervous exhaustion at home and let him get on with his second job here.

'That'll be me.' He carried on cleaning his paintbrushes on the dirty rag he'd pulled from his pocket and no one would ever have guessed he'd just turned her world upside down.

'You?' She waited for him to burst out laughing and tell her he was only joking, and that actually John, the elderly porter at the clinic, was her real partner. That would have been preferable to the thought that she was expected to spend the next weeks grinding up against the hospital hunk when the mere brush of his hand at her back had her jumping as if she'd been scalded.

'That's not going to be a problem, is it?'

Yes, it was going to be a problem! She could scarcely be in the same room as him without getting all hot and bothered and frustrated at herself for finding him attractive despite all those qualities that normally made her want to run in the opposite direction. Not only was he rumoured to be the workplace Lothario, but she'd seen him when things didn't go his way and she had no intention of inviting another volatile man into her life. She didn't want to be fooled like her mother and get hurt as a result.

Although none of what had happened tonight was making any of this easier for her. She didn't need to see a softer guy who did charity work and didn't get upset when she changed his plans at the last minute—that wasn't going to help her get over this nonsensical crush that made her pulse race every time their paths crossed. Neither was spending countless hours of rehearsal time pressed cheek to cheek and everything else up against him, but what choice did she have now? It was going to be pretty obvious the issue she had was a personal one if she pulled out now, and not the one he would probably assume. Retreating from the situation was just going to lead to more friction at work, since there was no way she could tell him the real reason she didn't want to be paired with him. She was in a no-win, no-escape-from-this-attraction situation. All she could do was hope it would end once the pressure of the competition claimed her attention.

'No. Of course not. I'm looking forward to dancing with you.' The lie burned her tongue. Her scars already felt as though they were shining out from beneath the tattoos, declaring her damaged goods in comparison to the numerous beauties he'd been linked to in the past.

She could imagine twirling around the floor, the raised skin where she'd been sewn back together mapping out the story of her life beneath his fingertips and making him recoil in disgust. It wouldn't be the first time a man had rejected her because of the way she looked, although she'd sworn it would be the last time anyone would have the opportunity to get that close. The dent in her confidence had been partially repaired with the magic of a tattoo needle, but even that only managed to disguise the trauma her body had gone through from a distance.

'Dancing? Who's dancing?' One of the elderly gentlemen who'd been pottering around nearby now sidled up to engage in the conversation.

'We're just talking about the competition, Grandad. This is Mollie, from work. She's going to be my partner. Mollie, this is my grandfather, Hugh Sheridan.' There really was no need for Ben to make the introduction as the family resemblance was obvious. Although the hair was a lustrous snowy white and the brilliant blue eyes surrounded by deep laughter lines, Mr Sheridan senior was basically an older version of his grandson.

'Nice to meet you, Hugh.' She reached out her hand to greet him but, rather than shaking it, he lifted it to his lips and dropped a kiss there instead.

'Lovely to make your acquaintance, Mollie.'

The old-fashioned flattery brought a flush to her cheeks and it was easy to see where Ben had inherited his charm from.

'I taught Ben everything he knows,' he said, with that same twinkle in his blue eyes she'd seen in his grandson's on her arrival.

'I'm sure you did.' There was probably a *Sheridan Handbook for Seducing Women* tucked somewhere between the family photos, she surmised, given how easily she'd already fallen for their routine.

'I was quite the mover in my day.' As if to prove the point, he tugged Mollie towards him, put her hand on his shoulder and began to sway. With one hand gently resting at her waist, he whisked her around the floor, moving so quickly it stole her breath away. He was such a strong lead, so adept, it didn't seem to matter she didn't know the steps to whatever song he was humming. Ordinarily she would've been mortified by the display they were putting on for the others in the room, but there was something reassuring in the confidence of her partner's steps that put her at ease. If Ben had indeed inherited his grandfather's skills as well as his looks, they might actually be able to salvage something of this shambles.

'Put her down, Grandad.' Although Ben was always delighted to see his grandfather having fun and being his old smooth self, he didn't want it to be at the expense of Mollie's comfort levels.

He'd been afraid to question what had prompted her decision to take part again for fear of scaring her off when she was clearly already skittish about participating. After their previous run-in it was a big step for

her to seek him out here, especially when she'd so ve-
hemently denied entering the competition in the first
place. He certainly didn't need his grandad scaring her
off again. Not everyone responded well to having him
around.

Hugh spun Mollie out with a final flourish that
sent her off balance in her peep-toe spotty wedges and
forced Ben to step in before she clattered into the nearby
metal shelving.

'Sorry,' Mollie mumbled into his chest as she col-
lided into him, her hands warming the skin beneath
his T-shirt. He was lost in those eyes staring up at him,
shifting from green to blue like the ever-changing tides.
He'd always thought her pretty but seeing her up close
like this, away from the work environment, he was free
to appreciate the beauty of her quirky style. Not only
did she look like one of those sexy fifties' pin-ups, but
she emitted that same look-but-don't-touch vibe. Especially when she was pushing away from him and putting
as much distance between them as possible. A detail
that could prove awkward for the purposes of her visit.

'You'll have to work on your showmanship if you
want high scores from the judges. They like a bit of
flair.' His grandfather was oblivious to any discomfort
he'd caused as he went on to critique his unsuspecting
dance partner.

'I'll remember that.' Mollie humoured the comment
with a smile and retrieved her red and black, cherry-
embossed bag from the floor where it had fallen in the
melee. She brushed the sawdust off it and Ben hoped
it wasn't one of those designer pieces that cost more
than a small car.

'Gran and Grandad were ballroom champions in
their day. They were the ones who taught me to dance.'

It had been an attempt to instil some discipline and respect into their wayward grandson. Like any sullen teen, he hadn't appreciated it at the time, but now those steps reminded him of that precious time he'd spent with people who'd loved him and genuinely wanted the best for him.

In the beginning Ben had thought engaging him in the fundraising efforts was a good idea since they were dealing with two areas very close to his heart. After this display he was beginning to think his involvement might turn out to be more detrimental than beneficial to the cause. Still, he wasn't doing this to win any glitter-ball trophies. At least here, under supervision, his grandfather was still made to feel useful, undertaking the less perilous tasks of sanding down the wood.

'Perhaps you'd be able to show us a few pointers when the time comes?' It was refreshing to find Mollie offering to involve his grandfather in the proceedings when so many often regarded him as a nuisance. Including his ex, Penny, who'd seemed to regard him as competition for Ben's attention.

That simple acceptance had his grandfather grinning from ear to ear. 'I like this one, son. She's much nicer than that last one.'

The slap he gave Ben on the back before he walked away whistling almost knocked the air from his lungs. It was as close to a compliment as anyone could get from him. These days he wouldn't be long making his opinion known if he found fault with anyone. Another reason he and Penny had found it impossible to even be in the same room together. He'd frequently commented on his dislike for her and Ben wasn't altogether convinced it had solely been down to his condition. With hindsight he'd concede her actions at times could've been considered selfish, especially when she'd given him the ultimatum between choosing her or his grandfather—a contest she could never have hoped to win. Ben owed him too much, loved him too much, to throw him on the scrapheap without a second thought.

Unfortunately, this unconventional introduction left him having to make an explanation to his work colleague about a part of his life he tried to keep private. He did his best to keep the details of his grandfather's decline in health since his retirement out of the public domain, but that secrecy had left Ben's own personal life open to speculation and exaggeration. A price he was more than willing to pay to preserve the reputation his grandfather had built over the years as an eminent local GP.

'Sorry about that. He didn't get along with my ex.'

'She didn't like dancing?' The droll reply managed to make him laugh and he appreciated the attempt to remove some of the awkwardness of having to discuss his personal life with her. He wouldn't have blamed her if she'd taken great delight in hearing about his failed relationship when he hadn't been the nicest person to her in the past, but it obviously wasn't in her nature to be malicious. It gave him hope that, whatever personal issues were uncovered during their time together in preparation for this competition, she wouldn't try to use them against him. Plus, that sense of humour he hadn't known she possessed might actually help make this experience less of a chore for them both.

'Not a fan of Hugh Sheridan's in general.' It occurred to Ben that he'd had no idea if Penny enjoyed dancing or not. In their eighteen months together he couldn't remember a time when they'd actually done it for fun. They'd attended all the usual evening functions together that demanded their attendance as representatives of the hospital, but she had always seen them as a way to make connections rather than an excuse to cut loose on the dance floor with him.

'Ah. Do you two come as a package deal?'

'Something like that.' He was reluctant to get drawn into the whys and wherefores of it all now, when the two of them were just beginning to get along. Any difficulties would probably make themselves apparent in time anyway and she'd realise why no other woman was willing to stick around for long. The very fact she was still here after that display was already an improvement on recent records.

'Well, uh, I look forward to dancing with both of you. Just tell me when and where.' She slipped her bag up over her shoulder and made a move to leave. Ben should have realised a young, beautiful woman had somewhere else to be. Not everyone spent their free time socialising with pensioners and volunteering manual labour. She'd look more at home sipping cocktails in an exclusive wine bar or whizzing along the coast in a convertible car than she did here in the grime and chaos of The Shed, but he wasn't ready for her to go.

They'd had that run-in at work but he liked that she'd challenged him, questioned how every course of treatment would affect her patient personally; it showed she cared. He'd slipped up that one time, becoming more confrontational than usual after a rough night trying to get his grandfather settled, but, now she was here laughing and joking and shedding that frosty image she unknowingly projected at work, he couldn't wait to start the lessons. It would do him good to be around someone younger for a change and remind him he hadn't totally surrendered his right to fun in order to look after those who needed him.

'We have a room upstairs we hire out for meetings and classes. No one's using it for the next few weeks so I thought it would be perfect for rehearsals.' It also meant he could split his time between The Shed and dance rehearsals without having to go home in between.

'Sounds good. We can compare work rotas and fig-ure out a schedule but I'm free tomorrow night unless any emergencies arise.'

'Me, too.'

'So I guess that means it's official then... We're doing this.'

He could see Mollie's apprehension in the way she was biting her lip and nibbling off a patch of that bright red lipstick until she was starting to make him nervous about the extra commitment he was taking on here, too.

'In that case I'll see you same time tomorrow then, partner.'

She stopped worrying her lip long enough to smile at him; an acceptance that no matter what challenges lay ahead they were in this together. In that moment he was prepared to clear his entire schedule to make time for her. And the competition.

CHAPTER THREE

MOLLIE HAD HAD a full twenty-four hours to obsess over the prospect of spending the evening ahead with Ben. That included several hours' sorting through the entire contents of her wardrobe deciding on what to wear. From all those eighties' dance movies she'd seen, the uniform for practice was supposedly a leotard and leg warmers, but that was a step too far out of her comfort zone and might have attracted more than a few curious glances on the Tube.

Instead, she'd opted for a pair of red Capri pants and a red and white checked shirt for ease of movement. She'd had the foresight to tie her hair up in a scarf tonight and donned a pair of rubber-soled baseball pumps in case she slipped, having seen how dusty the premises were last night. Outwardly, at least, she thought she looked the part, while the cha-cha-cha was going on in her stomach.

For anyone who didn't know better, they could've been forgiven for thinking she'd been getting ready for a first date. She shrugged off the ridiculous notion, putting it down to the teasing she'd endured from her sister over the subject. In the short time she'd been at the hospital even she knew about Ben's reputation as a ladies' man and seemed to think that was a cue for

Mollie to throw herself at him. As if some ill-advised affair orchestrated with a work colleague would erase all traces of her painful past.

It was silly to be thinking about this as anything more than a *show*-mance, a pretend partnership they were hoping would impress the dance judges and those willing to pay to see the spectacle. If only someone would tell that to her flip-flopping stomach and pounding heart, which were insisting this could be the beginning of some passionate love affair. That was as likely as this being the start of a glittering dance career, but sometimes it was nice to fantasise that the impossible could happen.

They definitely had a *spark*, and she wouldn't be human if she hadn't thought how that might translate onto a romantic level. They'd already proved they were both passionate when they needed to be and goodness knew he was easy on the eye, but she certainly didn't need any more complications in her life when she was trying to simplify it.

If living with her mother had taught her one thing, it was that relationships were anything but simple. However, unlike her other family members, Mollie's love life had never been a priority and she wasn't about to make it one now.

She could see the light on in the room above the darkened shop front and as Ben's tall shadow moved across the window upstairs it soon became apparent he was the only one in the building. It added an extra out-of-hours frisson that she really didn't need if she ever hoped to get these nerves under control. She let herself in and followed the music drifting down the stairs. It had that sensual beat that brought images to mind of sexy Latin dancers moving their bodies together like lovers and she immediately froze on the steps. She'd been so consumed by the prospect of this first appointment together it hadn't even occurred to her to worry about what dance they would actually be required to perform together.

She was a beginner; someone who wasn't particularly comfortable in her own skin, and she'd seen enough demonstrations of dance talent to know the dramatic, sultry steps required for a rumba or a tango, or, heaven forbid, a paso doble, would be her worst nightmare come true. Not that she could see herself shimmying and sashaying to a salsa either.

Why the hell had she agreed to this?

She took a step back, seriously considering tiptoeing back out of the door and pretending she'd never come here.

Unfortunately, the traitorous wooden step underfoot creaked with the shift of her weight and gave away her position.

'Mollie? Is that you? Come on up.' Ben peered down from the top of the stairs and stole away that last chance to back out.

'Hi.' She pasted on a smile and forced herself up towards a man most women would already be stampeding towards.

'I'm afraid I can't offer a sprung floor, or mirrored walls…' Ben waved her into the perfectly adequate space with an apology, but Mollie would take the inoffensive magnolia walls over her reflection staring back at her from every angle every time.

'I think you're overestimating my abilities here. I don't even know what difference that would make to whatever crime I'm about to commit against the soft shoe shuffle.' She dumped her bag and her jacket on the stacked seats near the door. The rest of the room had obviously been cleared to give them space to move around and, judging by Ben's rolled-up sleeves and the faint glisten of sweat on his forehead, it wasn't difficult to work out who had done the heavy lifting.

'Don't worry. Everyone was paired up according to their abilities. We didn't have the budget for professionals but we did partner those of us with some know-how with the novices. You said on your application you had no previous experience. I'm fully aware of what I'm in for.'

She wished she did.

'And as far as footwear goes, you will need to learn how to move in heels.' He eyed the sensible shoes she'd worn for practicality, prioritising her need to keep her bones intact over her sense of style for tonight. All to no avail, it would seem.

No leotard and leg warmers were needed for him to look every inch the part, standing there with his hands in the pockets of his well-fitting black trousers, the fluorescent ceiling light reflecting off his shiny black shoes and shirt opened at the collar to show just a hint of toned chest.

'I'll look forward to the demonstration,' she said, trying to play down how out of her league she was with an injection of humour. It might help her relax if she pictured him with his trouser legs rolled up showing off a pair of candyfloss-pink stilettos.

'That's lesson three.' That quick dry humour to rival hers made her laugh out loud. It was heartening to know he didn't take himself too seriously when they had absolutely no chance of winning this competition and it put her under less pressure to match whatever skills he possessed.

'I'll be sure to put that into my diary.' She stepped into the middle of the floor, fidgeting with her scarf while she waited for the moment when he took her in his arms and discovered all her inadequacies.

'I suppose we should get started then. We're performing a waltz. That's the dance my grandad demonstrated to you.' He walked over to the clunky CD player plugged into the wall to change the music to that of a less frantic tempo. It was the modern equivalent to dusting off a gramophone player in the day and age of downloads and phones with the world available at the touch of a button.

'Oh, good. I won't be expected to drag you across the floor with a rose clenched in my teeth then?' If he was as confident and capable as Mr Sheridan senior, she knew he'd lead and support her throughout the routine even though she'd have to work on that flourish at the end.

'You can if you like, but we might be penalised for illegal dance moves.'

'I like to live on the edge.' A blatant lie but she was sick of being the one known for sticking to the rules.

'That's not what I've heard.' Ben stepped forward, so close there didn't seem to be any air left between their bodies.

Mollie resisted the urge to take a step back now morbid curiosity and a need to get through this rehearsal as soon as possible were taking over from her attack of claustrophobia. 'Oh?'

'Okay, you're really going to have to work on your acting skills and at least pretend you don't hate my guts.' It was Ben who created a safe space for her in the end, his apparent exasperation driving him away again.

'I don't—' Clearly her acting was better than either of them imagined if that was what he thought.

'No? You'd think you'd just been given a death sentence, not that we're about to dance. Loosen up.'

'Sorry. I'll try.' She cricked her neck from side to side and shook out her limbs, willing the tension to leave her body along with any thoughts that weren't strictly ballroom related. The character assassination could wait for a while.

'We'll start that again.' He let her take a few breaths before he advanced again and attempted something as daring as moving her into position with him.

She could see that tic in his jaw as he ground his teeth together and it was more comforting for her to believe it was because he wasn't any more relaxed about this than she was, rather than profound irritation with her. This really wasn't going to work if she riled that temper again.

'The box step forms the main basic step of the waltz and we do it with a one, two, three count. Step forward with your left foot on the one, take a sidestep with the right, and close your left foot again to the right.' He glossed over any nonsense to demonstrate the move.

'One, two, three…' She watched his feet and tried to concentrate on replicating it to defuse the situation rather than overanalysing whatever it was he might have heard about her.

'Good. Then we go back with the right, sidestep with the left, and close the right foot to the left foot. Keep repeating so it feels as though you are marking out the four corners of a box.' It seemed so easy when he was doing it, his feet, and hips moving as though he didn't have to think about it.

Whereas Mollie was having trouble with the concept of even counting to three. 'Like this?'

'That's it. Now we'll try it in hold. Place this hand on my shoulder and put the other in mine.' He manipulated her frame into position until the palm of her hand rested on his solidly reassuring physique.

'Am I going forward or backwards?' She didn't think he'd be able to feel the raised skin of her scars through the cotton barrier of her shirt, but she was worried if she was expected to wear one of those fairy-tale gowns for the competition she'd look more like an ugly stepsister than a princess. A low-cut back or too-short hem would put her scars on show for everyone. It was inevitable she'd have to explain them at some point in the proceedings and endure the looks of pity and disgust. Until then she wanted to revel in this belief she was actually dancing. For the next hour or so she didn't want to inhabit the real world and instead let Ben carry her off into that magical world of make-believe.

'You're starting off on the back step. Ready? And… one, two, three…' He began the count and they moved in time to the music, her odd misstep no matter with such a strong partner.

Eventually she trusted the momentum enough to stop watching her feet, but lifting her gaze meant looking deep into those gorgeous eyes and almost forgetting what it was she was supposed to be doing here other than holding on to him for dear life. They were pressed so intimately together she should've been embarrassed but, unlike the few men who'd been this close, he wasn't expecting anything of her other than a willingness to learn. She wasn't afraid but the adrenaline was pumping around her body every time his muscles bunched beneath her fingertips. It was easy to see how people found romance in dancing, but she needed to remember he wasn't Patrick Swayze and she certainly wasn't a young girl looking for a holiday fling.

'Do I need to do all that head turning and bending over backwards to show the judges my teeth? It always looks a bit unnatural to me. Then again, so do the mahogany spray tans and impossibly high hair the TV dancers always have. I'm all for a girl looking her best but I draw the line at contortionism.'

This time she did make him laugh out loud, the deep rumble reverberating through her limbs, disturbing her equilibrium enough for her to step forward onto his toes when she should have been moving back.

'I can promise I won't be partaking in spray tans or backcombing my hair and we'll worry about the gymnastics later. For now just concentrate on the steps.' The rap on the knuckles came with a grin to take away the sting.

The need for heels soon became apparent as they shifted around the floor. Her steps felt flat-footed compared to the rise and fall of her partner's and she found herself tottering on tiptoe trying to match his easy rhythm. It was safe to say Mollie Forrester had finally moved out of her comfort zone and survived. She'd found something to make her heart race that didn't involve fixing other people. Right now she felt as though she was doing something fun for herself.

Ben needed the refresher lesson as much as his partner. It had been quite some time since he'd tripped the light fantastic and he hadn't seen his grandad dance since his grandmother passed away eight years ago. Her death from cancer had hit them both hard and even prompted Ben's move towards the hospital field he worked in now. Unfortunately, that time had also seemed to mark the beginning of his grandfather's health problems. Dancing with Mollie had managed to give them both a much-needed boost. He just wished she were enjoying it as much as he was instead of tensing every time he touched her.

'So, uh, what was it you heard about me that made you think I was a stickler for the rules?' The question had clearly been hovering on Mollie's lips since he'd let that slip. He knew how inaccurate and hurtful rumours could be and he should never have opened his mouth when it became apparent she was no more of an ice queen than he was a philanderer.

'It was nothing sinister, don't worry. I've simply heard it said you don't tend to socialise outside working hours or generally stand any *nonsense*.' That was the best way he could think to phrase it. She was friendly and efficient but it was thought she didn't like to stray too far from the rules. That droll sense of humour of hers could easily be misconstrued by someone who didn't appreciate it, but from his own experiences over these past couple of nights he couldn't help but wonder if it was her way of covering her nerves when she wasn't one hundred per cent comfortable in certain situations.

A paranoid partner was the last thing he needed when he was trying to get her to relax. She was already hesitant in the basic steps, as though she didn't have any confidence in her abilities to master the simplest move. Part of becoming a dancer was making it look effortless, as if you weren't thinking ahead to the next step or counting the tempo in your head. The last time he'd seen her absent of worry had been under his grandfather's influence. He wanted to see her happy and, more than that, he wanted to be the one to put the smile on her face.

Ben took a stride out of their assigned box area and began to spin her around the perimeter of the room.

'What are you doing?' she gasped, trying to keep up with him.

'Trying to get you to stop overthinking everything, to just feel the music.' They continued to cover the floor until the song finished and he ended the rogue routine with a dip.

'See, you're more flexible than you thought,' he said, tipping her back in an attempt to extract that same breathless laugh his grandfather had drawn from her. Instead, as Ben leaned over her, her lips parted in surprise and her eyes darkened with something more dangerous to his well-being than laughter.

The CD finished, leaving only the sound of their breathing to break the silence in the room. All logical thought had vanished from his head so he couldn't form a sentence even if he tried. How could anyone have believed this woman cold when the heat between them was making him sweat?

The shrill interruption of a mobile phone ringing thankfully saved him before the moment became even more uncomfortable for either of them. He snapped back upright, bringing Mollie with him.

'You should get that.' It was only when she pushed him back in the direction of the ringing, he realised it was coming from his jacket.

'Excuse me.' He was thankful for a reason to turn away from her so he could get his thoughts under control. It wasn't as though he'd never danced with a beautiful woman, but he hadn't anticipated an attraction to this particular partner.

He swiped his thumb across the screen to accept the call, his forehead creasing into a frown when he saw who it was calling.

'Hi, Amy. Is everything all right?' She'd been happy to stay with his grandfather tonight to leave him free for this dance rehearsal, but now guilt immediately swamped him with the notion something had happened while he'd been showing off up here with Mollie and thinking about how good she felt in his arms.

Sometimes he imagined this was what parenthood was like—stressful and impossible to escape once you'd committed to it. He'd become a father to a seventy-three-year-old man.

'Not really. I was making Hugh a cup of tea. One minute he was happily sitting watching TV and the next minute he was gone.' Anxiety quivered in Amy's voice and Ben's stomach dropped into the shoes he'd spent much too long polishing when goodness knew what had happened to his grandfather.

'What do you mean "gone"?' There were so many disturbing definitions of that word when associated with a man of his age, none of which Ben wanted to contemplate.

'The front door is lying wide open and I can't find him anywhere in the building. I'm so sorry, Ben. I only turned my back for a minute.' The hiccup in Amy's voice made her distress clear but none of this could've been anticipated. If either of them had imagined his grandfather wandering off a possibility they would've been more security conscious.

'Okay. Have you reported it to anyone?' They needed to think about this logically and take practical steps to find him.

'No. It's literally just happened.' Amy wasn't usually one prone to panic, which had made her the ideal candidate for the job in the first place, and Ben didn't know how he would cope without her.

'In that case he couldn't have got very far. Knock on the neighbours' doors and check if anyone's seen him and I'll jump in the car and take a spin around the neighbourhood. What's he wearing?'

'That's just it—he was only wearing his pyjamas and his slippers when I saw him last.'

That made him more vulnerable than ever. Not only did it mean he was in a more confused state than usual, but he was also exposed to the elements. Now the summer was at an end those cold, dark nights were beginning to draw in and flimsy nightwear was not adequate protection from the chill of September. Neither was walking the streets in his pyjamas the act of a man who'd always taken pride in his appearance, insisting a doctor had to look respectable to earn respect.

'I'll be there in five minutes. Don't worry, we'll find him.' He ended the call, aware that Mollie had walked towards him during the course of the telephone conversation. It would've been impossible for her not to have overheard, or get the gist of the crisis currently going on. Given the look of concern on her face, she wanted to help whatever way she could, but Ben had to make the decision whether or not that was one step too far into his personal life.

'Is everything all right?' Mollie touched him lightly on the arm in a gesture of support he wasn't prepared for but appreciated all the same. There hadn't been anyone else other than Amy to offer him any comfort recently and she was paid to help.

'It's my grandad... He's gone missing. I'm sorry, I have to go.' He didn't want to waste any time trying to think of a cover story when the basic facts gave him reason enough to turn the lights out and start locking up.

'Can I help?' Mollie shrugged on her jacket and jogged down the stairs after him.

'Thanks, but I'm sure we'll manage.' He'd learned, when it came to ailing pensioners, most people usually only offered their services out of politeness, so few following up on any promises it had become second nature to decline and save them all the bother of pretending. It was at this point alleged good Samaritans took their leave, conscience salved, never to be seen again. He hadn't expected to find her still standing on the pavement after he'd closed the shutters.

'Surely two sets of eyes are better than one? When and where was he last seen?' In complete contrast to last night when she couldn't seem to get away quickly enough, she followed him to the car park at the back of the shop. It crossed Ben's mind that perhaps she was one of those people with a knight-in-shining-armour complex—or in this case a nurse-in-shiny-red-lipstick—who simply thrived on being needed.

The uncharitable thought was quickly wiped from his mind when he saw her uploading a map to the phone in her hand. She was taking this seriously.

'At home.'

Mollie's frown was the last thing Ben saw before he jumped into the car. He could've driven away and left her wondering how on earth a man in his seventies could get lost in his own house. It would be easier than opening up and having to explain exactly what was going on in his life.

This dance thing was only supposed to be a bit of fun to raise money, not an invitation for someone he hardly knew to pry into his personal business. It was only night one and she was already showing an interest in the area of his personal life he guarded most closely. He was wary of letting anyone breach those defences again after Penny had so cruelly abandoned him and his grandfather when things got tough.

Yet he still found himself stretching across the car to open the passenger door for Mollie; that strong pull of wanting to have her near greater than his need for privacy in this moment of crisis.

She peeked her head through the door, as though still waiting for confirmation she was welcome to join the search.

'You're right, two heads have got to be better than one,' he conceded, trying to convince himself this was about what was best for his grandfather, not him.

'Does he live far from here? Could he be on his way here?' Mollie was already scanning the dark streets as she put her seat belt on and it wouldn't have been a bad theory if not for the fact he would've had to get on public transport to get here. Even in this day and age, Ben would like to think a frail man in his pyjamas would warrant some help in the city before he got this far. Unfortunately, the apartment was in a more secluded area where he might not be spotted so easily.

'I think it's too far for him to have come in such a short space of time.'

'Was that your grandmother on the phone? I'm sure she's worried sick.'

'No…er…she passed some time ago. That was Amy. She helps me look after him. He gets a bit…confused sometimes.' There really was no way of explaining this without referencing his grandfather's ill health otherwise he just came across as an overprotective control freak.

'Does he live on his own?'

'Not any more. He moved in with me just over a year ago.' He let the implication of that sink in as they drove ever closer to the place he called home. Far from the carefree bachelor he was rumoured to be, he was in fact a man with a dependent relative in tow. It was unfortunate that by revealing this snippet of information, he'd proved how inept he still was at keeping him safe.

'Wow. That must have been difficult for you.'

Ben shrugged. 'Not any more than it was for him. He's always been such a strong, independent man it wasn't easy for him to give up his home.'

It was frightening being ripped away from everything you'd ever known and deliver control of your life into someone else's hands. He'd gone through it himself as a kid, having to accept a sudden change of circumstance and leap into the unknown praying it would work out. It had taken faith and a lot of trust that someone who loved him would only have his best interests at heart and it was ironic—if more than a little cruel—that more than twenty years later the situations had been reversed. Ben only wanted to do the best for his grandfather, even if they could never hope to have the happy ending he'd had as a boy. Dementia would never allow it.

'I'm sure it wasn't but you two seem to be very close. He's lucky to have you.' Mollie met his eyes in the rearview mirror and a small glow of warmth crept into his chest, thawing out the cold fingers of fear that had been gripping his heart since receiving that phone call. He didn't do any of this for praise or sympathy, merely out of duty and love for his grandfather, yet that look of admiration made him sit taller in the driver's seat. This was the first time he'd shared the information with anyone who hadn't responded about how this would impact on *their* life rather than his. He suspected it would be a different story if they were embarking on a relationship other than one based on charity.

Ben gave a bitter laugh. 'I think it's very much the other way around. If anything happens to him…'

Even with the struggles they endured he couldn't imagine a life without his grandfather in it. It had been difficult enough saying goodbye to his grandmother, helpless to halt the progression of her illness then, too, but at least there'd been two of them holding each other up when grief had threatened to fell them. Without his grandfather he would have nothing. No one.

They circled around the neighbouring streets within walking distance of Ben's apartment but there was no sign of his missing relative.

'Is there anywhere he likes to visit? A park he and his wife used to go to? Or somewhere he feels safe? If he's confused he might look for something familiar.' For a woman who'd only met the man twenty-four hours ago, she sounded every bit as concerned as Ben was about his safety.

This was how he should have been with Penny: able to share his fears and find solutions without facing the prospect of blame and ultimatums. He could see now she lacked the empathy that came so naturally to Mollie. As, apparently, did the rest of his family. If he'd had anyone like Mollie on his side to share the weight of responsibility he might not have had to choose between family and a personal life.

Penny had known how affected he'd been by his parents' refusal to take responsibility for his, and his grandfather's, welfare. He'd trusted her enough to impart those deep-rooted issues and how he'd felt as though he'd been abandoned time and time again. Yet she hadn't thought twice of walking away herself when faced with the same commitments on her time and energy. She'd never taken his feelings into consideration when making that decision and had left him wondering for the second time in his life if he'd ever truly been loved at all.

In the space of a few hours Mollie had already shown him more support without even knowing his history. She was just as eager to run towards the conflict as Penny had been to get away from it and proved she was a better person than his ex. It made Ben want to confide in her and hope her sweet nature would neutralise the bitter taste of betrayal that had lingered too long.

'He doesn't generally travel too far unless Amy or I are with him. His memory isn't what it used to be any more.' They drove past the corner shop where his grandfather went for the morning paper every day but it was shut up for the night, with no sign of anyone except a teenage boy riding past on his bicycle.

The rain had started to fall and he hated to think of Hugh out here cold and alone, with no idea where he was. If they didn't find him soon there'd be no choice but to phone the police and report him missing. They would have the resources for a search on a much broader scale. Time would be of the essence now, before hypothermia or some other serious medical consequence of being out here set in.

'What about home? His home, I mean. Where did he live with your grandmother before moving in with you?' It was easy to tell her mind was working overtime trying to solve the mystery along with him, and this genuine concern for people she hardly knew was exactly what made her a good nurse. He was sure there was probably a good reason she seemed a bit distant from her colleagues and had gained an unfair reputation to that effect.

Perhaps she had an elderly relative tucked away at home that she had to get back to at the end of every shift, too.

'It's not too far. About five minutes away in the car. Although, I'm not sure he would remember how to get there under his own steam.' Neither of them had been back since the house had sold. It was too painful to remember the family the three of them had once been there before illness split them apart and forced them to leave the good memories behind.

'It's worth a try, right?' She could easily have cried off by now and left him to it, but here she was, winding down her window and leaning out of the side of the car for a better street view, regardless of the falling rain. Penny would've already been complaining about the havoc the weather was causing with her hair, or fretting about being left with water marks on her clothes. Although Mollie obviously took as much pride in her appearance, it didn't take priority over everything else. In his world it made all the difference when there was one less thing for him to have to stress about.

They trailed the route from his apartment building back to the house where he'd spent the best years of his life, with no success. He decided to do one last tour around the vicinity before admitting defeat and pulling over so he could phone the local police. A lot of these suburban streets looked the same in the dark, and especially to an old man who couldn't even remember where he'd left his glasses from one minute to the next.

As they turned around one corner, they found a large dark shape sitting hunched on the front garden wall of one of the semi-detached houses. The car headlights picked out the rain-drenched, pathetic figure of his pyjama-clad grandfather squinting against the light.

'There he is. Thank goodness.' Ben immediately pulled over and shut off the car engine so he was plunged back into darkness. The last thing he wanted was to scare him off like some skittish creature caught in the spotlight.

'Are you okay, Hugh? We've been so worried about you.' Mollie was out of the car first, taking a seat beside him on the wet wall and speaking to him so tenderly it could've been her own grandfather she was addressing. The cold that was no doubt seeping into her clothes didn't seem to bother her as she leaned across to put an arm around his shoulders and comfort him.

'I think I took a wrong turn.' Ben's grandfather glanced around at the unfamiliar surroundings, his whole body shaking and his teeth chattering. If he'd been out here in the cold for too long there was a risk of hypothermia setting in, which could quickly become life-threatening. Yet he didn't appear to register anything other than his poor sense of direction.

'Where were you going, Grandad?' Ben took off his jacket and draped it around his grandad's shoulders to protect him from further exposure to the elements as well as prying eyes. It was sad to see the fabric hanging loosely around his now bony shoulders, hunched over in defeat, with all that strength that Ben had relied upon in his youth now stripped from him physically and mentally.

'Home. Where do you think?' Hugh snapped, as though Ben were the one behaving erratically.

'We don't live here any more. Remember?' He hated these moments most of all. It was one thing having to remind him where he'd left his possessions, or that he didn't have to rush out of the door in the mornings to see his patients, but having to tell him time and again that his wife had passed away and he could no longer be trusted to live on his own was painful for both of them.

'Of course, I don't live here. I'm not stupid. I told you, I took a wrong turn.' As was the pattern his mood switched without warning with Ben being accused of playing tricks on him. That unreasonable, damaged part of his brain turned his loving grandson into a monster who was trying to drive him mad.

'It's late, Grandad. Why don't you come home with me and I'll get you some warm, dry clothes?' It was no use standing here arguing with him in the rain when he'd probably have forgotten this conversation by tomorrow anyway. The important thing was always to keep him safe and give him peace of mind over that logical need to get facts right. There was no need to cause him any more distress but there was a growing need to get him indoors. It was difficult to assess him out here when some of the symptoms associated with hypothermia—tiredness and irrational behaviour—had become such a part of his personality now.

Hugh resisted Ben's attempt to chivvy him towards the car, eyeing him with suspicion and that paranoia trying to convince him his grandson was a stranger trying to coerce him into going somewhere he didn't want to go.

'You can't sit out here all night, Hugh, you'll freeze.' Mollie took his hand, which was turning blue with cold, and Ben could see her subtly checking his pulse. If it became slow and weak they'd really be in trouble but, as she gave him a reassuring nod all was well, he hoped they'd got here in time.

'Where did you go, Ellen? I was trying to find you.'

His grandfather sounded so lost as he mistook her for his late wife, it broke Ben's heart that he would have to deliver the news to him all over again about what had happened to her. Some days it was a blessing he didn't have those nightmarish days spent on chemo wards or in the hospice with her as she fought for her last breath, but not tonight when that memory lapse was putting his health in serious jeopardy.

'Why don't we go back to Ben's place and get warm?' Without batting an eyelid at the mix-up, or the need to correct him, Mollie coaxed him over to the car.

'Are you coming, Ellen?' He hesitated to get into the back seat without her, distrust radiating from him towards Ben, who was holding the door open for him and trying not to take anything personally. The only way to get through these moments was to remind himself this was the illness attacking both of them simultaneously and not a true reflection of the relationship they'd cultivated over their years together.

'Sure.' Mollie slid into the back seat and held out her hand to encourage him to join her. Her ease with the situation immediately seemed to reassure Ben's grandfather he was safe and he didn't put up any further resistance as he clambered into the car beside her.

'What time is it? We don't want to keep Ben up late when he has to go to school tomorrow. We told his parents we'd look after him. We're going to get him back on the straight and narrow, aren't we, Ellen?' From time to time he did regress to those days when he believed the three of them were still living together, oblivious that Ben was a grown man now who no longer physically resembled his teenage self. The mind was capable of blocking out those important details in its confusion. That little titbit about his rebellious teens probably hadn't gone unnoticed by their lovely companion, but he was counting on her to be discreet about all of tonight's events.

'Well, then, we'd better get moving, hadn't we?' He slammed the door shut and jumped into the driver's seat, leaving Mollie to assist his grandfather with his seat belt since he seemed more inclined to accept her help.

Her ability to remain cool in a crisis, unfazed by tonight's turn of events, made her more attractive to him than the world's greatest supermodel. There was no question of her physical beauty, but he knew that didn't always reflect the true nature of the character inside and tonight she'd shown him who she was behind the make-up and rumours. It didn't match the detached partner he'd assumed he'd be dancing with and was causing him to think of her in a whole new, alluring light, which was no doubt going to make this arrangement less straightforward than he'd planned.

For now, though, his priority was to get his grandfather home safe and warm. As always, his personal life would have to wait.

CHAPTER FOUR

MOLLIE DOUBTED THIS was any more fun for Ben, or Hugh, than it was for her but a person would have to be made of stone not to be moved by their plight tonight. Ben had given her opportunity to leave from the minute he'd got the news his grandfather had gone missing but she'd been happy to help. With Talia home there was no need for her to race back and she could never have left Ben to deal with this on his own anyway.

She knew what it was like to receive one of those emergency phone calls that meant you had to drop everything and run to help. She'd done it time and time again when her mum had phoned drunk from a club disoriented and needing someone to come and find her. Although her mother's self-inflicted state of confusion wasn't the same as an elderly man's clear distress, she was able to sympathise with the toll it would take on Ben being called out tonight. Especially when he didn't seem to have anyone else to count on to help. Sometimes having that extra person to share the burden with made all the difference. Someone who was able to say, *You're not alone.*

Her presence here seemed to be helping Hugh settle, even if he was a bit mixed up about who she was. She hadn't pretended to be 'Ellen' but she hadn't corrected him and neither had Ben. Hugh was obviously having trouble grounding himself in the here and now and she wasn't going to achieve anything by insisting she wasn't who he thought except make an already difficult situation worse.

'Is everything all right back there?' Every now and then Ben would glance back at the two of them and she could see he was worried about what was being asked of her as well as his grandfather. He needn't have worried; if there was one woman who was used to babysitting her elders, it was Mollie.

'We're fine, aren't we?' She patted Hugh's cold hand and flashed him and his grandson a smile to put them both at ease. A lifetime of making sure the people around her were happy often contributed to her volunteering for duties she wouldn't normally entertain, including this dance competition, but she genuinely wanted to help because Hugh had seemed such a lovely man when she'd first met him. That change in his behaviour had come as a shock to her so goodness knew how Ben had coped with it.

'We're nearly home now.' Ben carefully navigated the car through a series of turns when Mollie knew he probably wanted to get his grandfather home as quickly as possible.

As they pulled up outside a block of swish apartments more fitting for an eminent young surgeon than an elderly man in his pyjamas and slippers, Mollie could almost feel his relief.

'Let's get you inside.' She unbuckled both of their seat belts and didn't have to wait long before Ben came to assist them from the back of the car.

'Have you got homework to do, Ben? We don't want you falling behind again.' Hugh clutched onto Ben's arm, giving a further glimpse into the kind of relationship they'd had even in their younger days.

She couldn't imagine a time when Ben wasn't the confident, capable man he was now, but it did sound as though his upbringing hadn't been as straightforward as people might have imagined. Whatever the mysterious history it was obvious he'd at least had someone looking out for him and she knew how important that was to a child when that support had been missing from her life. Despite being a twin and having lived with her mother for most of her life, she'd always felt alone in her fight to make things right at home. At least Ben and Hugh had been able to rely on each other at one time or another.

'No homework tonight, Grandad,' he said without any sighing or contradiction, making it clear this wasn't the first time they'd gone through this routine.

Mollie wondered how many alarming conversations they'd had where Ben had reminded him he was a surgeon now before he'd accepted there was something wrong. She'd dealt with enough elderly patients to know it could be some time before families realised there was more amiss than simple forgetfulness and how devastating it was to have their lives turned upside down by illness. It was tough to watch loved ones wither away to someone you no longer recognised. Worse still when you were the one to blame for stripping away the person they'd once been.

She didn't imagine illness was any easier to accept and live with than guilt.

There was an unspoken agreement for her to accompany them into the apartment and she followed Ben through the opened door.

'Oh, thank goodness you're okay.' A small, motherly

figure rushed towards them the second they stepped through the front door.

'We found him out near the old house. Sorry we worried you, Amy.'

'I'm just glad you're safe but look…you're all soaked through. I'll go and get you some towels.' She bustled off and returned a short time later clutching a bundle of towels and a dry pair of pyjamas for Hugh.

'Amy, meet Mollie from the hospital. My new dance partner.' Ben introduced them as he passed Mollie one of the towels from the stack. The woman's eyes were wide with surprise at the news and it was hard to tell if it was because it was a colleague or a dance partner he'd brought home. Since he was supposed to have quite the collection of conquests at work, Mollie assumed it was the latter.

'Lovely to meet you. I wish it had been in better circumstances.' If it hadn't been for bad timing, she would probably never have had reason to set foot in here.

'I'm going to go and help Grandad get out of his wet clothes. Thanks for staying on, Amy, but I can take it from here. You go on home.' Ben replaced the jacket around Hugh's shoulders with a dry towel and ushered him down the hall.

'I'll make sure they're both okay before I leave. If you have a mobile phone I could take your number and give you a text later.' The least Mollie could do was send a message and make a cup of tea if any of them were going to rest easy tonight.

'That's so kind of you. Thank you. I only live a few streets away so if there's any problem at all just give me a call.' They swapped numbers and goodbyes at the door before Mollie went into the kitchen to hunt for the kettle.

Any of her actions tonight could've been seen as

presumptuous, but it was always at the forefront of her mind that if she were in Ben's shoes, she'd appreciate any form of help. She took three matching mugs from the cupboard and set out a plate of chocolate biscuits she'd found, grateful someone in the house had a sweet tooth. It had been impossible for her to eat very much today when her appetite had done a vanishing act in advance of their supposed dance rehearsal and now she was paying the price. She was munching on the biscuits trying to appease her grumbling stomach when Ben walked into the kitchen.

She choked down a mouthful of crumbs as she was caught helping herself. 'Sorry. I didn't have any dinner before I came out tonight.'

'You should've said and I would've ordered us a take-away.' The way Ben devoured several of the digestives as though he'd inhaled them suggested he hadn't taken time for dinner either.

'This will keep me going until bedtime anyway.' She slid a mug of tea along the worktop towards him before taking one for herself. 'There's a cup for Hugh, too, if he's coming out.'

Ben shook his head. 'He's fast asleep already. Tucked up under the blankets like a baby. I think all the excitement and fresh air tired him out. Thanks for your help and for playing along with the whole Ellen business. That was my grandmother he mistook you for. Sometimes he forgets she's not with us any more.'

'I guessed as much. Does it happen often?'

'This is the first time he's wandered off but the memory lapses are becoming more common. I'm probably going to have to get some sort of live-in carer from now on. I can't afford to take any chances of him doing that again, especially when I'm on night shift. I want to keep him out of a care home as long as possible. Without his support when I was young, I could easily have ended up in foster care or a juvenile detention centre the way I was going.'

'I know it's not easy. Do you have a relative who could help out? It's a lot to take on all by yourself.' There was another nod to the fact his childhood had been every bit as dysfunctional as hers but she didn't want to pry into what had happened. She was sure he wouldn't want to go into detail about it any more than she would about her childhood. What mattered now was the great person he'd become in wanting to do right by his grandfather. With any luck he had a brother tucked away somewhere who would step up the way Talia had.

The option obvious to an outsider would be to find a retirement home that could take care of Hugh full time but Mollie knew handing over responsibility wasn't as easy as signing a few papers. If so, she would've moved out of home and left her mother and sister to fend for themselves a long time ago.

Mollie had been almost institutionalised by the demands of caring for her mother and it was likely the same for Ben. He probably couldn't imagine anyone else taking care of his grandfather and showing the same care and affection as family when she was even having trouble handing over the reins to her own sister.

'I'm an only child, so no brothers or sisters to call on for help, I'm afraid. Not much in the way of family at all except for my parents and they, uh, travel a lot. They would rather see him go into a home than tie themselves down with the commitment of looking after him. It's fine, though. I've got Amy. She's a good friend. What about you? Any family?' Ben asked, apparently reluctant to share any more about his circumstances.

'I have a twin sister, Talia. She's a nurse, too, just started at the hospital in the emergency department.' She was on edge as he studied her face, probably trying to figure out a family resemblance to someone he might have been acquainted with in the department. The rain and exertions of the evening had most likely removed all traces of her make-up and left her completely exposed without her usual carefully perfected exterior.

'Non-identical,' she pointed out as she turned away to rinse her cup in the sink.

'It would be difficult to imagine there could be two of you out there.' Ben came towards her to place his empty cup in the sink.

'Is that a good thing or a bad thing?' Her voice became a breathy acceptance of him encroaching into her personal space as he reached around her to turn the tap on.

'Oh, I don't think the world is ready for two Mollie Forresters. Not when the one we already have is so amazing.'

It was no wonder he never seemed to have trouble finding a date when he had that way of melting a girl's common sense. Even though she was standing here looking like a drowned rat, he was saying all the right things and looking at her as though she really were the most beautiful woman in the world. It was a shame it was certainly a well-rehearsed routine.

Mollie cleared her throat and her mind as he stepped back from her again. 'I'm nothing special. Talia is the force to be reckoned with.' She managed to stop herself from adding that Talia was the pretty one, the fun one and the sister men always preferred because that would've sounded like an attempt to garner sympathy even though every word of it was true. It wouldn't be long before he ran into her and realised it for himself anyway.

'Ah, but does she have your incredible sense of rhythm?' He held out his hand and beckoned her towards him.

'I would say Talia's dance style leans more towards street than ballroom.' Her sister did everything with such gleeful abandon she couldn't imagine her taking to the discipline and elegance of old-fashioned dance, whereas the rules and routine were easier for Mollie to get a handle on than the idea of performing for an audience. That said everything about the differences in personalities between her and her sister. One wild and free, with the other unwilling to stray too far from convention.

'She doesn't know what she's missing then, does she?' He stepped forward and Mollie had no hesitation in taking his hand and letting him whirl her into position. Although her heart still raced at his touch, the palpitations came more from the thrill of being so close to him than the anxiety of her inexperience. As they immediately moved into the box step they'd rehearsed earlier she found herself eager to learn more about the dance, and the new feelings this man had inspired in such a short space of time.

After seeing him in action tonight both as a dance partner and as an anxious grandson looking out for his family, she trusted him to lead her into the next stage. That belief in him was a bigger step for her than any new waltz move.

'Definitely not.' And Mollie wouldn't be able to tell her about this time as they laughed and twirled around the kitchen floor to the dance track playing only in their heads. Talia would either find it lame or read way too much into it and Mollie wanted to preserve the special moment like this in her head for ever.

When he was spinning her around and carrying them towards the living room there was no chance for thoughts of her mother or sister to settle in her head, with only room for thoughts of her next step.

Unfortunately, she made the mistake of looking into his eyes instead of where she was going. He was so focused on her face, as though the sight of her alone was enough to spur his movement, Mollie was thrown off her count. In her panic to make sense of it she stepped back when she should've put her foot forward, compromising their once solid frame.

Mollie took a blow to the backs of her knees as she blindly walked back into the furniture, knocking the air from her lungs as she toppled onto the unseen sofa, bringing Ben down with her. Now there was no escaping that penetrating blue stare when his eyes were only millimetres from hers and his lips a fraction away. There was no mad scramble to untangle from each other, as though lying sprawled here on top of one another was perfectly acceptable. She wasn't sure whose heart she could hear pounding in her ears when his breathing was every bit as heavy as hers.

There was no reason to fight the kiss when it came so naturally, as though part of the dance, and she continued to follow his lead. He leaned closer, she closed her eyes, and, for the few sweet seconds his lips were on hers, let herself believe she was desirable. Wanted.

That was before she remembered who and what she was beneath the camouflage and what the next step could lead to when it wasn't part of the assigned routine. The time for him to find out for himself would come soon enough without inviting ridicule or revulsion. She'd heard all the comments before but that didn't make them any less painful.

With her hands on his chest she levered enough pressure to break the seal between their mouths even though her body was crying out for more of his attention.

'I should probably go.' Her voice was husky with the desire that wouldn't abate simply because her brain had interrupted that primal response to the sexual chemistry they'd somehow managed to create. She'd heard it said before the close contact required for a believable connection between dance partners often lead to explosive, if short-lived and ill-advised, affairs and now she was finding out first-hand how easy it was to get carried away. Even though beautiful blondes like her sister were supposed to be much more his type.

She was probably little more than convenient to a man like Ben. It wasn't his fault he wasn't aware she was that lesser known species of thirty-one-year-old virgin.

The second the kissing stopped and the talking started, it hit home for Ben that he'd stuffed up on a multitude of levels. There were so many things wrong with this scenario he didn't know where to start backing away from it but that didn't mean he hadn't enjoyed acting on impulse with Mollie. According to certain body parts beginning to stir, he'd enjoyed it a bit too much.

It was a natural reaction, especially when there was a beautiful woman kissing him back, but Mollie had since made it clear a line had been crossed and she regretted it. If Ben had been thinking logically himself he would never have given into desire. Instead, he'd let himself get caught up in the exhilaration of that simmering attraction. Just because his pulse had gone into overdrive at having her warm body pressed so intimately against his, it didn't mean he'd had to act on it. He'd spent the months since Penny had left resisting temptation and he didn't know what made Mollie the exception.

He wondered if it was down to the incredible compassion she'd shown towards his grandfather, which made him see her in a different light from the other women he'd spent time with lately. Although he should be used to the tribulations of caring for someone with dementia, tonight had been a particularly trying time. It marked another milestone in his grandfather's declining mental health, which was leading them both ever closer towards that dark alley from which they could never return.

The only glimmer of light in the shadows had been Mollie, so calm and understanding he'd found strength in having her by his side tonight.

Not to mention that every time he danced with her he was transported to another place, another time, where romance was alive and kicking and not merely a one-way ticket to heartache. He'd never had to worry about keeping his emotions in check any time he'd danced in the past, and this pairing had totally backfired on him in terms of keeping that distance he'd wanted to maintain between this competition and his personal life. One lesson in and he'd already kissed her as well as led her right into the middle of his chaotic home life. He mightn't even have made that move if not for seeing that same desire reflected in her eyes.

Now that he'd surrendered once to that sweet indulgence it was going to be a test not to do it again, but her decision to leave was probably for the best. They were colleagues who would still have to see each other long after this thing would burn itself out, and getting involved with anyone right now was a bad idea when all his time and energy were devoted elsewhere.

'If you're sure.' Despite his own reservations that continuing this was madness, she'd been kissing him back; all those anxieties buzzing in his head like a swarm of angry wasps were finally quietened.

'I should really get home…' Mollie shifted herself from underneath him and got to her feet.

Ben didn't want to prolong her obvious discomfort any longer than necessary. Hopefully with a little space she'd eventually forgive him and they could get back to simply being dance partners. 'Sure. Sorry.'

'It's okay. We've had a trying night and I think our judgement is a little off kilter. I think we should stick to the dancing from now on.' She straightened her clothes and patted her hair into place so there was no trace of evidence left behind that she'd done anything other than bust a few dance moves tonight before she walked out of the door.

On this occasion it was easier to believe those ice queen rumours, when she was able to remain so cool about what they'd done and he felt as though a tornado had just ripped through his life and thrown it into even more chaos than ever.

CHAPTER FIVE

'I DIDN'T HEAR you come in last night.' Talia sidled up to Mollie as she waited for the kettle to boil. She couldn't function the rest of the day if she didn't have her first morning cup of tea. Unfortunately that meant she was easy prey for nosey sisters until then.

'Didn't you? I was pretty tired so I just went straight to bed. I didn't know you were waiting up.' Mollie added an extra cup as she made the tea, realising the last time she'd done this was for Ben. That had been prekiss. Before he'd set her body on fire and turned her whole world upside down.

He'd had no business putting his lips anywhere near hers and she'd had no business responding as though passionate affairs were a frequent occurrence for her. She was never going to follow up one sofa-bound clinch with anything other than paranoia over her scars and how he would react to them. Apart from the glaringly obvious differences in their attitudes to relationships, she was serious about finally getting the space to live her own life and that certainly wasn't going to be enhanced by getting involved with another carer. If anything last night should've shown her a glimpse into her future if she didn't escape that prison she'd built for herself here with her mother.

'I thought maybe you'd stopped over somewhere for the night...'

Mollie could see Talia's smirk out of the corner of her eye but held her resolve and fought the blushes threatening to redden her cheeks. For the first time she understood her mother's predilection for falling in lust so easily and confusing it with something more powerful. There had been no rational thinking involved when Ben had fastened his mouth onto hers, only primal response.

'What kind of dance lesson lasts all night? Wait, don't answer that.'

This time Mollie did blush as even more carnal images of what could've happened during the course of the night on that sofa popped into her head.

Talia snorted and spilled some of her tea as she carried it over to the kitchen table.

Mollie joined her and although she would have liked to have someone to confide in about what had happened, she'd spent so many years dealing with things on her own it was difficult to suddenly start sharing her innermost secrets. It was going to take a while to strengthen that sisterly bond again and in the meantime she'd remain selective about the information she shared. Particularly because she hadn't figured out what to make of what had happened between her and Ben herself, or how to proceed.

'I didn't realise how...intimate this dancing lark would be. I mean, I knew we'd have to get up close physically but I found it all a bit overwhelming, to be honest.'

That small admission was apparently sufficient to throw Talia off the scent of anything juicier as she turned her attentions towards the box of cereal sitting opened on the table and helped herself to a handful of dry golden flakes. 'It's bound to be a bit awkward at first. Did you enjoy it, though? Eventually?'

Mollie tried to remain focused on the waltzing aspect of their evening and there was no question that she'd got into the swing of things before everything had become so surreal and confusing. Every step she'd taken with Ben in that stuffy room had been a release away from the stresses in her life. Right before she'd added one more significant one.

'It wasn't as bad as I imagined. Ben's a good teacher.'

'Ooh. Ben, is it?'

'Very mature.' Mollie sniffed as they descended into childish teasing.

'I'll bet dancing isn't the only thing he's good at. It's all about the hips…' Talia shovelled another handful of flakes into her mouth, oblivious to Mollie almost choking on her tea.

It wasn't as if she hadn't thought the same thing, having felt his passion for more than just the quickstep. 'He got called away to a family emergency so we had to end the rehearsal early.'

She could've elaborated on the heartbreaking details of the family circumstances that had diverted their energies away from the competition, but that would have been a betrayal against Ben. He'd been reluctant enough to accept her help on the matter, a proud man wishing to keep knowledge of his grandfather's health to a minimum. It was a privilege that he'd granted her access to his circle of trust and she would respect the honour afforded her. After all, she wouldn't want details of her troubled personal matters tossed around in conversation for entertainment either.

'That's a shame. I was hoping this was the start of a beautiful friendship. Or, you know, a sultry affair.' Talia teased her with a flirty wink and made Mollie even less inclined to fuel her fantasies by revealing that kiss to her when she wasn't sure it meant anything other than they'd got carried away in the moment.

'What is the fascination with trying to get me hooked up with someone? Are you on commission with a lonely hearts club somewhere for every sad singleton you get signed up?'

'Is it so wrong for me to want you to be happy?' The playful sister immediately transformed into the pouting teenage version.

'Of course not, but I don't need a man in my life to make me happy. I'll be quite content with a little flat of my own and control of the TV remote. You'll be pleased to know I have a viewing appointment later for a flat closer to the hospital.'

'Good. I'm glad you're taking some of my advice on board.'

'And you're really okay with me moving out?' Although they'd discussed the possibility, it would be a big change for all of them and Mollie was afraid it might prove too much.

'One hundred per cent. I've told you, I'm staying put from now on. I need to put down some roots.' Talia ripped off a piece of the cereal box and shredded it into tiny pieces of anxiety confetti. It didn't take a psychic twin bond to figure out there was something wrong.

'Why? Is there something going on I don't know about?' Mollie had grabbed at the opportunity of independence when the subject had first arisen; she hadn't really given any thought as to what had really brought her sister home.

'I guess I'm not going to be able to hide it much longer... I'm pregnant, Mollie.'

It wasn't the bombshell she'd been expecting but it left her stunned nonetheless.

Her sister was going to have a baby. She was going to be an auntie.

Mollie immediately dashed around the table to give her a hug because she could see for herself just how much the thought of becoming a mum terrified her sister. 'This is good news, right?'

'I'm not ready for this.' Tears were dripping down Talia's face now as the enormity of her situation fully hit home.

'Hey, you've always got me. We'll get through this together.' Now wasn't the time to ask about the father, when she'd made it clear he wasn't in the picture.

Talia wrestled out of her grip and wiped her eyes with the back of her hand. 'That's exactly why I was supposed to wait until you'd moved out before I told you. This is my mess. You've covered for me here long enough. I can't keep expecting you to pick up the pieces. We both know what kind of mum that would make me to this baby.' Her fears of ending up like their own mother, who was still asleep upstairs, oblivious to the life-changing revelation going on in the kitchen, were well founded. Absentee parents, missing in their kids' lives either physically or mentally, did not make for nostalgic childhoods. They would both do whatever they could to prevent that happening to another generation.

'Is that why you're so keen to get rid of me? So you can turn my room into a nursery?' Mollie was only half joking, when Talia's insistence she could manage her mum and the house on her own made even less sense now Mollie knew about her predicament.

'I've travelled, I've had my fun and now it's time I grew up and accepted my own responsibilities.'

'You're making it sound as though you're a hundred years old and ready to lie down and die, not a young woman about to embark on the biggest adventure of her life into parenthood.' A baby was an incredible responsibility but it was also something to celebrate. Mollie didn't want her to think this was the end of her life when it was the start of an exciting new chapter for her.

'Believe me I've thought long and hard about what I'm getting myself into and that's why I'm positive you should still move out. I don't want to be the one who keeps holding you back. If you're still here when the baby comes, you know you'll never make the break. It's not as though we're never going to see each other, and perhaps Mum and I might both be finally forced to step up if we stop relying on you to fix everything.' This was the most maturity she'd ever displayed and yet Mollie couldn't prevent anxiety burrowing deep into her skin at the prospect of leaving these two to fend for themselves.

'And if you can't manage Mum and a baby?' It was all well and good telling her to move out and take on her own place with her own bills, but if Talia decided one day she couldn't handle it after all and took off again, Mollie would be the one left to pick up the pieces.

'I'll just have to, won't I?' It was exactly that lack of foresight that gave Mollie serious second thoughts about keeping her viewing appointment later. Sure, Talia had good intentions now, but there was no coping strategy in place, no carefully thought-out 'what if' plan to cover all eventualities. That was probably how she'd ended up alone and pregnant in the first place.

With more coercing from Talia, Mollie did go to see the flat in the end and it was on her mind during rehearsal.

Now she was more torn than ever about leaving home. Okay, so it needed a deep clean and the smell of grease from the chip shop below lingered in the air, but it was the independent lifestyle it represented she found attractive. Along with the price. Thanks to her private practice outside the clinic—tattooing eyebrows for cosmetic as well as medical reasons—she'd managed to put away a small nest egg. Unfortunately London house prices wouldn't allow her to rent anything more glamorous than a one-bedroom flat so she'd never been expecting to move straight into the home of her dreams.

'Your head's really not in the game tonight.' Ben hopped around in a circle as he worked through the pain of having his foot stamped on for the umpteenth time that night.

The one benefit there'd been in worrying herself sick over the situation at home was that she'd been too consumed by it to leave any space for worrying about coming here tonight. Whether or not she moved out of home, there was absolutely no room for anyone else in her life. No matter how good a kisser.

That didn't mean it was easy to continue these lessons as though nothing had happened. Mollie tried to look anywhere other than his face, so close to hers— that dark smudge on the wall where someone had left a dirty fingerprint in the fresh paint, the mirror-like shine on his shoes—but her whole body was tense with awareness now she was back in his arms.

She was a bundle of nerves again, trying to get her head around the new steps he'd shown her, but it was difficult to concentrate when there were so many new feelings and emotions zinging through her body every time she came into contact with Ben.

He'd awakened a part of her she'd thought she'd shut

down for ever—that desire to be with someone so great it overshadowed the possible consequences. Every time she faced spending time with him she was pumped up with the anticipation of seeing him and fear of how he was changing her. Until he'd shown an interest in her that seemed to go beyond duty, she'd accepted the idea of being alone, content to simply move out of home. Now she was constantly thinking about the alternative and how much more fulfilling her days were with him in them. They had a real connection, which seemed to cross over into their personal lives as well as their professional ones, and it meant a lot having someone who could relate to her circumstances without judgement.

There was also that overwhelming urge to have him kiss her again, which she couldn't shake off and she didn't know what to do about it. It wasn't as though she could keep her distance, given the reason they were here, and if she was honest it was contributing to this growing sense of panic threatening to consume her. This was a lot of new ground for her to get used to all at once and she wasn't managing any of it effectively.

Ben was right: neither her head, nor her heart, were committed solely to dancing tonight.

'Sorry. I've a lot on my mind.' She broke frame, dropping her arms to her sides along with any pretence she could carry this off. There were a lot bigger decisions for her to make other than which way to spin next. If the worst came to pass she'd simply let Ben trail her around the floor on the night of the competition, because she had more faith in him than she did in herself right now. The consequences of her next steps outside this room could have serious repercussions for everyone around her, and that was enough pressure without the worry of publicly embarrassing herself on the dance floor.

'Look, I'm sorry if I made you uncomfortable last night. I'll understand if you want to back out of this.' Ben quickstepped away from her to turn off the CD. They didn't really need the song playing anyway, when Mollie could hear it in her head and picture the steps every time she closed her eyes.

It took her a second to work out what he was referring to, because *uncomfortable* wasn't the word she associated with what they'd done in his apartment. Passionate, surprising, exciting maybe, but never uncomfortable. She hadn't known how to respond to the situation then any more than the one she found herself in now. If she walked away now she knew she'd come to regret it. This was supposed to be the beginning of her independence and doing things she wanted to do. Despite all her anxieties, she knew she'd have a harder time giving this up than seeing it through. Dancing had brought her a lot of pleasure, as had kissing Ben, and she didn't want to deny herself the opportunity of either happening again. The prospect of something more happening between them, regardless of the palpitations it induced, was also strong motivation to continue.

'How is your grandfather?' She purposely misinterpreted his meaning so she could delay analysing that kiss a bit longer.

Ben took a few beats before he said, 'Fine. He's a bit more subdued than usual but Amy's spending the day with him.'

Mollie took a swig from the bottle of water she'd brought in with her. The cool liquid couldn't quench the new thirst she'd developed over the course of the past twenty-four hours but it would have to do. It was definitely the less complicated option.

'I'm glad he's okay. I couldn't stop thinking about you, him, last night.' Mollie swallowed her Freudian slip down with another mouthful of water. He didn't need to know her last thought before drifting off to sleep had been that clinch and what could have been.

'I'd be grateful if you could keep it all to yourself.'

She almost spat out that last gulp of fresh spring water again as she read between the lines. If they weren't going to carry on from where they left off, then he didn't want his reputation tarnished by being romantically linked to her. 'Of course. I haven't said a word to anyone.'

'It's just… It's private, you know? I'd rather keep family details out of the workplace. He doesn't have much of his dignity left and I'd like to preserve whatever I can for now.'

'Your secret's safe with me. I know only too well how important it is to keep the two separate. If people knew the half of what went on in my house I doubt I'd be allowed to practise.' So she was exaggerating a fraction, but she'd always imagined if people knew the stresses she'd been through they would think her work might be compromised in some way, and kept herself to herself as a result.

Ben raised his dark eyebrows at the revelation. 'You have a wild side I don't know about?'

Flashes of that wild side from last night came to mind, when she'd abandoned all thoughts of convention in favour of acting recklessly for once, but he knew all about that. 'Not me.'

'Ah, that famous sister of yours? I'll have to meet her some day.'

'Unfortunately, I have my mother to contend with, as well.' She'd wouldn't normally let details of her home life slip out so easily, but since she'd seen his for herself there seemed little harm in letting him know he wasn't the only one dealing with family problems. Sometimes the knowledge you weren't alone in your suffering was enough to get you from one day to the next.

'She's a bit of a handful, too?'

'You could say that. She…she doesn't manage very well on her own. That's why I had to get back last night. I didn't want her to worry.' It was an excuse for running out so her lack of experience wasn't so blindingly obvious.

'You live with your mother?' He tilted his head to one side, probably thinking how quaint, or sad, that was for a grown woman. Somehow living with a sick, elderly relative seemed nobler than staying at home because of the guilt you'd caused your parents' divorce and your mother's subsequent descent into self-destruction.

'Not for long. Now Talia's back she's going to take over some of the responsibility. In fact, I went to view a flat only today. It won't be long before I'm living independently and not having to worry about what either of them get up to.' She was rambling in her effort to convince him there was more to her life than baby-sitting grown adults, or, at least, there would be soon.

'That sounds nice.' He nodded his head, a sadness moving across his features, which she recognised as a longing for that same freedom. She'd worn a similar expression every time she'd waved Talia off on one of her adventures.

'Well, there's nothing set in stone yet. I'm just looking at my options. I got some news today that's actually making me rethink the whole idea.'

'Anything I can help you with?'

She hesitated in spilling the family secret so soon but after tonight's disastrous performance she reckoned she owed him an explanation. Besides, she needed someone to talk to about her situation who wasn't family.

She gave a sigh before she let go of the secret. 'Talia's pregnant. You won't say anything in work, will you? I don't think she's told anyone else yet. I'm not even sure she's told the father—'

'Wow. That's big. Your secret's safe with me, though.' He smiled as they entered into a pact never to discuss each other's personal lives and Mollie was glad now more than ever she hadn't said too much to Talia about what had happened with his grandfather.

'Thanks. It's a relief just to say it out loud and admit I'm as terrified as she is about the idea of a baby coming.' She'd offered nothing but support to Talia on hearing the news, but inside she shared all the same fears.

An awkward silence fell around the room and she began to castigate herself for oversharing. He had enough of his own problems to deal with without listening to hers. They were only supposed to be here to dance, for goodness' sake.

'Who's next? Anyone?' he continued, glancing over his shoulder as if he expected to see someone else gate-crashing their rehearsal.

'Are you expecting someone?'

'I was just waiting for the next member of the support group to pop up and introduce themselves.' The teasing smile softened Mollie's bristles and stopped her from taking offence.

'We are a pair, aren't we?' There were very few who understood the struggle of caring for family, seeing it as the duty of a daughter, or a grandson, with no notion of how much energy it took to keep that family ticking over. It was nice to be able to get things off her chest with someone who knew what she was going through.

'I reckon we deserve some time off. Fancy playing hooky for the night?' The mischievous wink should've tripped her self-preservation alarm, which activated every time someone asked her out, but he wasn't just any man and she knew he didn't have a hidden agenda when he'd already told her he wanted to forget their last *lapse*. She was sure he was simply as worn down as she was with the constant stress of doing the right thing.

'What about rehearsal?' As tempting as it was to ditch one of her responsibilities for a while, she didn't want it to come at the price of later humiliation when her lack of practice became obvious to everyone paying to see them dance.

'We'll catch up. I promise. No one's expecting us home for ages and I think we both deserve some time off, don't you?'

She wasn't sure they'd put in enough work here to qualify as a full rehearsal, but they'd definitely earned a break from real life for a while.

'Do I need to change?' With those long legs, Mollie matched him stride for stride along the street as he hurried towards the lights beckoning in the distance. That fantasy land he knew was waiting out there on the heath was the first place he'd thought of when the need to escape reality for a while had become too great for either of them to deny.

He gave her outfit choice a cursory glance, even though the dark denim skinny jeans clinging to her curves and mint-green buttoned-down sweater were indelibly inked on his brain for the foreseeable future. 'You're perfect.'

It was obvious neither of them was in the right head space to get involved and yet he'd given into carnal temptation and almost ruined the bond they'd forged. Perhaps if this had come around at a different time in their lives they might have been able to pursue this connection they had. There was undeniably a mutual attraction and she *got* him more than anyone had since his grandparents had taken him in. In different circumstances they might have made the perfect couple, but he would never have the chance to find out for certain. There was no point getting involved in another relationship when outside commitments would never permit a happily-ever-after ending.

He was glad she'd still felt able to confide in him about her family situation and hopefully he'd repair whatever damage he'd done to their relationship with this impromptu night out. They might even manage to squeeze in some practice here, working on their balance, or at least helping them to relax around one another again without the shadow of that kiss making things awkward between them.

The Ferris wheel came into sight long before the smell of fresh popcorn and candy floss reached them.

'A funfair?'

He could see the layers stripping away until she was a child again, free from stress and responsibility and keen only to take part in the festivities. Exactly what he'd hoped for.

'A *vintage* funfair, organised by the local church to raise funds for their overseas charity work. We helped make some of the stall signs at The Shed.' He'd been proud they'd contributed in some part to the cause but he hadn't thought beyond making a donation person-ally. However, when it had become clear Mollie was too distracted to rehearse he'd thought this might be a good place to escape for a while. His instinct proved correct as she ran ahead, fitting in so seamlessly with the glamour and excitement of the spectacle.

'Oh, Ben, it's fantastic!' She planted a swift kiss on his cheek when he caught up with her, and though he was sure she'd left a glossy red imprint there he couldn't bear to wipe away any trace of her. He wanted to cap-ture a small part of her joy for himself.

'I can't take any credit except for the top coat on a few of the signs.' It wouldn't be fair to those who'd worked so hard behind the scenes to pretend he'd been involved beyond a paintbrush and a tin of varnish.

'But you thought to bring me here and that's enough.' She raised her hand to his cheek and the sound of laugh-ter and music in the background faded away as he held his breath and waited for her next move. Until she'd wiped away the lipstick mark and walked away he hadn't realised just how much he'd wanted to kiss her again.

The sway of her hips in those tight jeans and high heels had brought her to the attention of many in the lo-cale but Ben's attraction went much deeper than clingy fabric and flattering shoes. He'd found a kindred spirit in Mollie, someone who understood the complexities of his relationship with his grandfather and still wanted to spend time with him. For him, she was a reminder of what was missing in his life and what he could still have from time to time—fun.

This past couple of nights in her company had made him think about the demands on his time that were all for the benefit of other people. Although the dancing had started out as another obligation on behalf of The Men's Shed, Mollie had made that time enjoyable on a personal level. She was a threat to that packed schedule that had kept him too busy to think about his disastrous personal life, because now he could see what he was missing out on. The temptation to make changes in his life for that same freedom she was striving for was huge if it meant they could spend more time together.

'Two, please.' He paid their admission at the booth to the man in the flat cap and braces, who ripped off a couple of coloured paper tickets from the roll in his hand.

Mollie looked more at home here than the stallholders all dressed in vintage attire. Even in the midst of this loud, brightly coloured chaos she stood out—a genuine individual in a crowd of costume-wearing wannabes.

'Okay. Pick a ride.' Despite the beard, Ben looked so young and carefree eyeing the gaudy rides with glee it made it difficult for Mollie to imagine he'd been anything but adorable in his youth. Yet he'd hinted that he'd been a bit of a tearaway. The type who would've probably caught her sister's attention when they were kids. Talia was the one with a penchant for bad boys. Not Mollie. Her daredevil days had passed long ago and all she'd craved since was stability. Tonight might be a little…off-track, but it certainly wasn't anything either of them needed to lose sleep over.

'This one!' She headed straight for the gilded carousel in the epicentre of the fête first so they could take a turn on the exquisitely painted horses with the cheerful organ music playing in the background.

This was just what Mollie needed. She couldn't remember the last time she'd acted like a kid, free from the restraints of enforced maturity. Probably before the accident, when her family was coherent and she'd happily gone off to play, safe in the knowledge they'd all be there when she went home again.

Ben helped her down when the music came to a stop and led her over to the red and yellow stalls where cuddly toys hung from the canopies and the eager cries of, 'Roll up! Roll up!' greeted every excited passer-by.

At the test-your-strength booth he unleashed a primal grunt of male testosterone as he swung the hammer and hit the target. With Mollie, too. She had to admit to a certain territorial pride as the bell rang out and notified to all in the vicinity that he'd succeeded in displaying his masculine prowess.

It had been her call to cool things off last night, but that had sprung mostly from fear of the strength of her own feelings in the moment rather than lack of interest. She needed to make it clear in her head what exactly it was she wanted from this relationship with Ben before she got too carried away. As much as he made her want to explore her sexuality with him, it could ruin what they already had together. Her insecurity versus his experience had disaster written all over it if they ventured further than a kiss. Yet spending time with him, getting to know him and having fun together made her want to. It was that heart-pounding test of her vow not to get involved with a man again that made it so difficult to think of him only as a dance partner. Especially when he'd made it clear he was open to the idea of more. Until she was brave enough to risk her heart again she was content simply to be in his company and accept the inner turmoil it seemed to unleash.

'Okay, Mr Universe. You win the right to choose the next ride.'

'I think I need somewhere to recuperate after that.'

He dabbed imaginary sweat from his brow before he led her over to the Ferris wheel and well and truly wiped the smile off her face.

To him it was probably the most sedate of all the rides but to her it was the ultimate torture device. She glanced up at the height of the wheel and instantly regretted it, black dots swimming before her eyes and her stomach already behaving as if she were on it. A fear of heights was a common enough phobia but having actual experience falling from that altitude and having the marks to prove it gave her extra reason to be afraid.

She knew if she explained the problem to Ben he would understand and never dream of making her go up there. Yet being with him gave her the strength to want to face her fear. He wouldn't let anything happen to her and the nostalgia of the place, and the chance to act out romantic scenes she'd only seen in the movies until now, made Mollie want to put the past behind her.

She took several deep breaths before she took a seat beside him in the pistachio-coloured carriage built for two, and it was quite pleasant sitting under the canopy, swaying in the breeze. At first. As soon as the attendant locked them in and her feet left solid ground, her breathing became more rapid and she began shivering uncontrollably. She had no desire to make a scene but she'd trained her brain so well over the years to recognise possible danger and avoid getting hurt again it was difficult to break the habit.

'Are you okay?' Ben leaned across to check on her—presumably because she'd become a lovely shade of green to match the decor—but the shift in weight set them swinging again. She clutched onto the cold steel rail for dear life as they travelled ever upward, the sights and sounds becoming more distant below them.

'I…er…have a bit of a problem with heights.'

'Why on earth didn't you say? We could've done something more tranquil, like the bumper cars.' He was trying to distract her by making her laugh, but she was concentrating on not falling out and landing on some unsuspecting carny.

'I don't think I realised until this moment. Shouldn't we have seat belts or something? Health and safety exist now even if they are trying to be authentic.' The panic began to expand in her chest, threatening to block her airways. The last time she'd climbed this high…well, she'd come crashing down to the ground very quickly and her whole life had changed beyond recognition.

'Hey, look at me.' That authoritative tone she heard him use at work forced her to focus on him rather than the people turning into tiny specks below.

'Sorry, I—' Any words died on her lips when she came face-to-face with him and saw concern for her furrowing his brow rather than irritation. He didn't need to say anything at all to show her he understood her fears and how vulnerable she felt up here when it was written all over him. He cared about her.

'Deep breaths. In and out.' He held her hands and demonstrated the cleansing breaths he wanted her to take with him, inhaling great lungsful of air, which she was then supposed to let go with all of her worries.

She tried but the pictures were strobing through her mind so vividly she felt she was right back there running across the roof, jumping between the buildings until that first loud crack and the world gave way below, leaving her falling so helplessly to her fate. Her scars ached with the memory of those glass daggers slicing through her skin like paper and left her gasping for breath.

She was slipping in her seat, Ben's face swimming before her as the world around began to fall away and let darkness creep in. Terror had a tight grip around her heart, refusing to let go even for him.

'Don't you dare pass out on me. I know you're stronger than this fear. You just have to believe it, too.' He tilted her chin up with his finger, insisting she keep looking at him.

'Deep breaths,' he repeated, and placed her hand on his chest so she could feel the steady rise and fall of his. She took a shaky breath in, concentrating on his solid reassurance beneath her fingertips. Eventually she fell into sync with him, the steady rhythm helping to keep the panic at bay for a while.

'I promise you're safe with me.' Once he was sure she wasn't going to faint on him, Ben put his arm around her and pulled her away from the side of the car, close to his chest. It was only when she began to relax into his warmth that the shaking began to subside.

She clung to Ben, the safety of his broad chest beneath her cheek, much preferable to the world outside this car. In his embrace she felt safe and warm and a lifetime away from that nightmare from the past. 'Sorry. I'm being daft.'

It wasn't often she put herself in the position to face these fears head-on and relive the nightmare, but in the excitement of the evening she'd believed it impossible to be scared.

'Not at all. We all have our fears. Mine is clowns. I swear if one shows up down there you won't see me for dust.' He gave an exaggerated shudder and clung tighter to her.

'So much for living dangerously.' She buried her head

in the crook of his arm, hoping she'd never have to come out and show herself again after that neurotic display.

'Don't be so hard on yourself. There's no rule that says we have to do it all at once. We can spread it out a bit.' Ben gave her another squeeze, and this time when her heart gave a little leap it was at the prospect of another night out with him and not because she thought she might take a tumble out of this ancient contraption.

'You mean do this again?' Her pulse went wild at the suggestion he wanted to move their relationship somewhere beyond duty. She wanted to spend more time with him; it was what that might lead to that made her nervous. Mostly because he was the only man in a long time who'd made her consider the idea of taking things to the next level. She never had to be on her guard around Ben. He seemed willing to take things at her pace, not putting her under any pressure, and that made him all the more attractive. If and when she was able to face her other great fear and let him see her scars, she knew he would never do or say anything to hurt her.

Another night with Ben was a very tempting prospect and another chance to break further out of her comfort zone.

'I'd like to, if that's okay with you?' He held eye contact with her and Mollie knew he was asking her to be more than just friends.

That thought chased away any residual fears in favour of romantic fantasy. 'I'd love to,' she said with a longing sigh.

The car jolted and immediately brought her back to earth with a bump.

'I think we'll try and swerve any aerial acrobatics next time.' Ben held her closer and she had no reason to protest. Even though the stuttering start and stop of the ride as they let people on and off had her digging her nails into the palms of her hands, she was comforted by the fact he didn't let go of her even as they reached the highest point of the ride.

The wind whistled around them and Mollie closed her eyes and took deep breaths so she didn't do something crazy like try to get out or hug Ben so tightly he'd pass out. When she opened them again it wasn't to find the ground hurtling up towards her, it was a gentle descent giving her time to appreciate the beauty of the world around her and the man beside her. She was no longer in danger. She was calm. She was alive. She was safe.

'That's probably for the best. I had an accident in my teens, which I apparently still haven't come to terms with.' Even saying those words was more than she'd shared since the fall and it had only happened because of the support he'd provided this far.

'Are you okay?' Ben's jovial tone changed immediately she made her trauma apparent. It wasn't that she was seeking sympathy; the need to speak about it had suddenly become too great for her to keep inside any longer.

'I thought I was.' She tried to smile through the tears that had suddenly welled up from somewhere deep inside, along with the admission of how much she was apparently still suffering.

'Oh, sweetheart. I'm so sorry.'

Simply having someone acknowledge her pain was enough to tip the tears over the edge, even without him resting his forehead against hers as though he was trying to transfer some of that hurt away for her. Now that she'd opened the lid all that emotion was bubbling up inside her until she knew she had to let it out or implode from the sheer force.

'It's not your fault. It's not anyone else's fault but my own. I was doing a stupid dare…thought I was impressing people by larking about on the roof of a building. Well, they don't put up those warning signs for no reason. The roof collapsed… I fell…and spent months in and out of hospital. I ruined my life…and everyone else's.' She backed away and swiped her hand over her eyes. She didn't deserve sympathy for what she'd done.

'Hey. It was an accident. We've all made mistakes at that age and you've paid dearly for yours. I was no angel myself and I'm sure there's still some graffiti sprayed about to prove it. We're different people now compared to those kids we were then. By coming up here you've just proved what a strong, brave, beautiful woman you are.'

He was saying all the right things and Mollie wanted so badly to kiss him for his understanding, but she knew she was too emotional to be thinking straight. She'd shared a huge secret with him but she couldn't bring herself to tell him about the injuries she'd received. That was a step too far and a sign she hadn't quite reached that level of trust with him yet. They mightn't be the same stupid kids but she still had the same scars. It was going to take time for her to admit it.

They finished the ride in silence but Ben kept her in his embrace until they'd reached the bottom and even then he only let go of her to help her out, as if in the course of that one rotation of the wheel she'd suddenly become some fragile creature he was obliged to protect. While it was nice to have someone taking care of her for once, she didn't want him to see her in that role. If she told him all the gory details of the accident she knew she'd just become a victim to him, and she'd been enjoying being normal for one night enough to know she wanted to do it again.

'Do you want to grab a coffee or something stronger to settle your nerves? I can phone home and let them know I'll be a bit later than planned.' He seemed every bit as reluctant as she was to end this evening and go back to reality but Mollie didn't want to monopolise him any more than she had already. They should end the evening on a high note before any family emergencies interrupted and spoiled what, up until she'd had her freak-out, had been a perfect time out.

'I think we should probably call it a night. I'm wiped out after that.' She was afraid spending any more time together would result in more oversharing and cost her the chance of him following up on that promise to do this again some time. Not only was he great company, but it was refreshing to be with someone who didn't need anything from her. She wanted it to be the same for him and didn't expect, or want, it to turn into a counselling session every time they met up. It was way more fun acting like two naughty kids bunking off school together, and goodness knew she needed more of that in her life.

'Sure. I'll walk you back to the apartment and get the car so I can take you home.'

'Honestly, there's no need. The Tube station's on the way back to yours and I'm sure Amy will be glad to hand over the reins.' She wasn't ready to go back to his place in any capacity again. If this was how he usually seduced women, she could guess what that next step meant and she obviously wasn't ready to go there yet, if ever.

There was a tiny flicker of something across his face

she tried to convince herself was disappointment but he didn't try to talk her out of going home alone. However, gentleman that he was, he did insist on accompanying her to the station.

'Same time tomorrow at The Shed then?' She was already looking forward to seeing him again.

'It's a date.' Ben leaned in and gently kissed her on the cheek. An innocent enough goodbye, if not for his hesitation to leave and the crackling tension she could feel arcing between them with that one touch.

'It's a date.'

Those three little words carried her on the journey home in a state of euphoria, which helped her make the decision she'd been putting off too long. It was time to start prioritising her wants and needs and they definitely included Ben Sheridan.

CHAPTER SIX

THE DOORBELL SOUNDED from downstairs, quickly followed by hammering on the door. 'That'll be dinner. I took a chance you hadn't eaten tonight again and ordered takeaway.'

The decision hadn't only been down to Ben's empty stomach and a lack of time in between his engagements. He'd been looking forward to spending more time with Mollie and wanted to prolong rehearsal as long as possible. Last night had been the best time he could remember having since his grandparents had both got sick; a glance into the *normal* life of a carefree bachelor who didn't have to worry about how his date would react to his personal circumstances.

He'd be a fool to try and convince himself he didn't want more than a few casual dates with Mollie. She was different from Penny and every other woman he'd come into contact with since his grandfather had taken ill. At least he thought she was, given the way she'd handled the challenges thrown at her so far. It turned out she was just the same when it came down to commitment. She was never going to consider something serious with him when she was working to escape her family, but the time he spent with her reminded him of the man he used to be before duty took over. Perhaps they didn't have a future as a couple, it was too much to expect even from a woman like Mollie, but he could still enjoy some quality time with her.

Ben didn't wait for praise on his forward planning or a denial that she was even hungry before bounding down the stairs to answer the door. Tom was working overtime on some commission pieces that could generate a lot of income towards paying for mentors and materials and if he wasn't quick enough the man mountain might help himself to a slice or six.

'Pizza delivery!' Ben returned with the large cardboard box of sustenance, untouched by dusty Tom hands, and Mollie was quick to drag a few chairs over, using one as a makeshift table.

'My hero.' She certainly seemed to have worked up an appetite to rival his as she helped herself to a large slice of pepperoni.

Normally if he was trying to impress a girl dinner would be gourmet and somewhere more salubrious than a dusty room above The Shed, but Mollie had already seen past the flashy facade and he didn't feel as though he had to pretend he wasn't an eating-pizza-with-your-bare-hands kind of guy. He didn't have to impress her because she already knew who he was and was comfortable with him enough to confide in. It was a relief being in her company and taking time out from being Ben the surgeon, or Ben the carer, to simply be Ben for a while. That seemed to be enough for her and there were very few people in his life who accepted him for who he was rather than what he could do for them. It meant a lot to him.

'So you have some big decisions to make in the not-too-distant future?' It made a change to talk about someone else's family problems other than his own, even if there was a small chance they might overlap somewhere along the line. This dance competition appeared to fall somewhere in between that work and personal divide, as they'd already discovered. With their time so tightly split between family and career, finding time out for themselves was never going to be easy.

He didn't envy Mollie's situation with her sister, but he did wonder what it would be like to have that chance to opt out without his conscience suffering in the process. If he'd had a brother, or family of any sort who'd shown an interest, it wouldn't have had to be all or nothing—living with Ben or a nursing home. Not that he could blame Mollie for choosing life when he'd waved goodbye to his in order to look after his grandfather.

'The idea of taking that final step and actually moving out is terrifying. I'm worried about leaving Talia to look after a baby *and* our mum. Yet, that one-bedroom flat was so quiet...' She paused, slice of pizza halfway to her mouth, staring off into a world where there were probably no crying babies or chop saws buzzing and disturbing the peace.

'You have to do it.' Ben chomped down on the gooey cheese-covered crust without an ounce of remorse. It wasn't very often he got the opportunity to indulge his naughty side and he was enjoying encouraging Mollie to do the same on a much grander scale. She deserved to do something for herself and get out while she still could when Ben was sure she'd given so much to those around her.

'Yeah?' Her eyes sparkled with that meagre encouragement to give into temptation and it was easy to get caught up in her excitement.

'How often do you do something without thinking about how it'll impact on everyone else?' If she was anything like him the answer would be never and being that altruistic could often be a lonely place.

'Uh...' The fact that she even had to think about it said it all and Ben wondered if anyone appreciated the sacrifices she'd probably made along the way.

'Ben! Help!' The urgent yell coming up from the shop floor below cut through his daydream and the blaring siren of alarm immediately had him on his feet, reacting as he'd been trained to do in an emergency. Mollie was close behind him, her medical instinct to help just as strong as his.

Tom, who'd been cutting lengths of wood on the mitre saw the last time he'd seen him, was now slumped on the floor, all colour gone from his usually ruddy cheeks. He was holding up his left hand, blood running down his arm and pooling in the sawdust on the floor. It didn't take a medical expert to put two and two together and figure out what had happened. The combination of power tools and fragile body parts always came with a risk.

He slammed off the power to the machine to prevent any more accidents before he checked to see how much damage Tom had done to himself.

'Stay with me.' Ben knelt by the chair, clicking his fingers to keep Tom's attention. It was vital to establish the extent of the injuries before the shock of the accident or excessive loss of blood caused him to lose consciousness.

'It's my own stupid fault. I remembered to put my safety goggles on to protect my eyes but thought it was a good idea to stick my hand in the saw instead of the wood. Health and safety will have a field day with that one.' His breathing was becoming more measured now as the pain probably kicked in and he tried to push through it.

'Accidents happen. That's why we've got a first-aid kit on the shop floor. As you very well know, sharp blades and old men are an insurance nightmare.' Ben prised the good hand away from the one that was profusely bleeding to investigate the injury. The nod to the green box on the back wall was all it took for Mollie to swing into action and start unpacking all of the first-aid supplies they were going to need to patch Tom up so they could get him to hospital as soon as possible.

Ben wiped away as much blood as he could to find the source of the bleeding and stop it. If Tom had hit an artery they had no time to lose in case he bled out. It was every wood shop nightmare come true but Ben was just glad they'd been on site to help. It didn't bear thinking about if Tom had been here alone. From now on he was going to insist they introduce a new rule so no one was ever here on their own so they could avoid risking a repeat with even more serious consequences.

As expected, the cut was deep. His hand sliced almost to the bone. Even if they were able to save his fingers, it was most likely he'd severed tendons. If that connection between muscle and bone was severed he could still lose the use of his hand. To a hard-working man such as Tom, that would be the end of his world, and those he helped on a daily basis.

The rubber-band-like tension in the flexor tendons, which were close to the surface of the skin, often needed surgical repair in such instances.

Ben didn't keep a tendon hammer on standby and had to improvise with his own fingernail to test the sensation in Tom's fingertips. 'Can you feel that?'

There was no reaction as Ben pressed hard and with

the nerves in the fingers so close to the tendons it was possible the wound might have damaged them, as well. If blood vessels had been cut Tom would lose blood supply to his fingers, too. He was going to need surgery.

'I'm not gonna lose the hand, am I, Doc?'

'You have some tendon damage. The quicker we can get you to hospital, the better you'll recover.' He helped Tom elevate the hand above his heart so gravity would help minimise the blood flow as the heart pumped up towards the injury. Once the bleeding had slowed a little, he covered the wound with gauze and wrapped the hand tightly with a clean bandage from the kit.

'I'm already speaking with the paramedics, Tom. They'll be here soon.' Mollie tucked her phone under her chin to relay information to the dispatcher about his condition, letting them know he was still conscious and breathing on his own. With such significant blood-loss there was always a risk of the patient going into shock. The interruption of normal blood flow cutting off oxygen and nutrients to cells could lead to organ damage or even death if left untreated and it was helpful to have another trained professional who could keep a check on the possibility. She wrestled the goggles off his head and checked his pupils for signs of dilation, so Ben was free to focus on stemming the bleeding.

'How are you feeling?' It seemed an absurd question to ask a man who'd almost sliced off his own hand but it was necessary to continue the evaluation on his condition until help arrived. A person in shock could deteriorate quickly and the longer treatment took to establish, the greater risk of permanent damage or even death.

'Dizzy. The room's spinning.'

Mollie unfolded the foil blanket from the first-aid kit to wrap around him and maintain his body temperature before she checked his pulse and provided an update over the phone. The blood pressure was a little lower than Ben would prefer but it was only to be expected in the circumstances.

Tom closed his eyes as he veered on the brink of consciousness. He'd lost a lot of blood.

'Stay with us, mate.'

Sirens wailed somewhere in the distance and Ben slapped Tom gently around the cheeks, trying to keep him awake so they could get him into the ambulance as soon as possible. This was a time-sensitive injury and the extent to which he recovered use of his hand would depend on how quickly they could get him into Theatre to operate and repair the damage.

Mollie ran to the door to wave the paramedics in the right direction and relayed an update on their patient's condition the second they stepped through the shop doorway. Once they'd checked his obs for themselves again and established it was safe to move him, they transferred him to the back of the ambulance.

'You should go with him.' Mollie echoed Ben's own sentiment that he really ought to ride with him and be there for the handover to the ER consultant, but it wasn't as simple as that.

'I need to lock up.' He was stretched in too many directions by his responsibilities and it was only in times of crisis he realised how little give there was left in him. In making a decision to go with his patient in his professional capacity, he was letting so many other people down. Including Mollie, who hadn't signed on for anything other than helping charity and she'd even disputed that at one point.

'Where are your keys? I'll lock up. Don't worry I've got everything in hand.'

'Upstairs in my jacket pocket. Thanks, Mollie.' The paramedic closed one of the ambulance doors so for one brief moment the image of Mollie standing waving him off was framed perfectly in the other. It was a beautiful sight, which he was sure would remain with him for a long time. He'd find some way to make this up to her, but until their next meet he was determined to make the most of the help and try not to worry about anything except Tom tonight.

It was only when they were at the hospital he realised he'd left his car and house keys behind, along with his phone, and he was stranded here for the time being. Not easy when he knew tendon repair wasn't usually regarded as emergency surgery and the longer his friend had to wait, the more scarring could develop on the ends of the severed tendons and reduce the range of hand movement in the future. That would be a devastating blow to Tom and everyone who benefited from his leadership at The Shed.

Although he'd handed over Tom's care to the emergency department's consultant, who in turn had referred him to a hand surgeon, Ben was unwilling to leave recovery to chance and put in a call of his own. Derek Hancock was a well-respected expert in that field who'd been his mentor during the early years of his experience as a general surgeon, and agreed to come in and perform the surgery straight away as a favour. On condition Ben would assist. He wasn't about to say no when it gave him a chance to see for himself exactly how successful Tom's surgery would go.

He'd already scrubbed in when Derek arrived, looking very apologetic. 'I'm sorry, Ben, I've been called to an emergency. A seven-year-old boy is on his way in after a car accident. He's lost the fingers on his right hand and I'm sorry but that has to take priority over this case.'

'I understand. We'll have to postpone.' He was gutted that Tom was going to have to wait after all and that extra time could put him at risk, but he knew each surgery was judged on a case-by-case basis.

'Not necessarily. You have experience and you're an excellent surgeon. After all, you learned from the best.'

'You want me to do this?' Ben hadn't considered that option because Tom was a friend. Then again, as far as anyone knew he'd simply accompanied this patient en route to the hospital and that omission of information was better than waiting until another surgeon was available.

'You don't have to but you've got the green light to go ahead. Listen, I'll have to run. Let me know how it goes.' Derek left him to make the decision for himself but he was right, Ben *could* do this and he would, for Tom.

It wasn't a lengthy procedure but Ben was feeling the pressure as he extended the wound across Tom's fingers so he could locate the damaged tendons. He desperately wanted to do the best for Tom but hoped their relationship wasn't clouding the judgement of his own abilities. When the doubt began to manifest in beads of sweat forming on his brow he thought of Mollie and the trust she'd put in him over these past days. She'd obviously had a rough time but she'd been confident in him as a medical professional, and as a partner, to do the right thing by her. That faith was enough for him to set aside any second thoughts and focus on fixing the mess Tom had got himself into. There was no other option than for this operation to be a success when too many people were relying on it.

With the tourniquet tied around Tom's arm to temporarily cut off the blood supply, Ben was able to locate the ends of the severed tendons and bring them together. It was a delicate process to loop small sutures around the tendons and pull them together without bunching, which could cause stiffening in the fingers, but he remained mindful of how each stitch could impact on the future quality of his patient's life. He made sure there was adequate tension in the repair before he closed the wound with considerable relief. It would still take some time to heal and recover normal function but he was satisfied he'd done everything possible to enable that process.

Even as he came to the end of a trying night, one that wouldn't end until he found some way of getting home, his thoughts were still with Mollie and how much he really wished he were going back home to her.

Rather than wait for Ben's return, Mollie headed back into the street where the bustling sounds of the London traffic drowned out the thoughts in her head. Primarily, she'd been worried about Tom's injury, but the constant pull of attraction between her and Ben was insisting she stopped ignoring it.

It was the past holding her back from acting on her feelings, but she couldn't seem to stay away from him either. She was torn between her head and her heart, and all those other body parts that were telling her to go for it. This sexual awakening he'd created was something she was curious to explore but it also made her terrified at the same time. Even her unhappily single subconscience was demanding to know what she was going to do about the significance of that kiss they'd shared.

The simple answer to that was nothing for now, except fulfil the promises she had made to him. When she'd trekked back up to the eerily silent rehearsal space upstairs to retrieve their belongings she'd had to search his jacket pocket for the keys needed to secure the room. It was then she'd realised his car key was still hanging on the bunch and it wasn't immediately obvious how he was going to get back to his apartment when his car was parked at the back of the building.

Not only that, the unexpected weight of his blazer had also revealed he'd left his phone behind, too. She'd pulled the shutters down on the shop front while debating whether she should make her way to the hospital to return his belongings, but figured he was resourceful enough to make his way home somehow. That didn't stop her hopping onto the train in the direction of his house rather than her own.

'Hello,' she called softly as she let herself into the apartment in case Hugh was still up and thought she was an intruder.

There was no answer and a note from Amy left on the coffee table, presumably for Ben, confirmed his grandfather was fast asleep in bed. She folded Ben's jacket over the arm of the nearest chair and set his keys next to the note so he'd see them when he came in.

It hadn't been her intention to stay but, knowing Hugh was here alone and Ben had no way of getting into the apartment without disturbing him, she didn't have much of a choice. She caught sight of herself in the mirror and groaned. Her clothes were stained with Tom's blood and she didn't feel comfortable sitting here all night with that knowledge. Neither did she want to upset her mother or Talia by turning up looking like a victim from a horror film.

She eyed up the washer and drier and wondered if she would be taking liberties by throwing her clothes in the wash. It was one thing agreeing to let her lock up The Shed for Ben, but he hadn't handed his keys over so she could make herself at home in his apartment.

If she was quick he would never have to know and chances were he wouldn't be home this side of dawn. Tom was his friend and Ben wasn't the sort of man who would abandon him in his hour of need.

She slipped into the bathroom and closed the door as quietly as she could behind her, partly because she didn't want to disturb Hugh wherever he was in the house but also because this felt a lot like trespassing.

The bathroom was littered with Ben's grooming products and she couldn't resist lifting the bottle of aftershave perched on the shelf. As she closed her eyes and inhaled the familiar scent it brought back memories of every second she'd spent in his arms, pressed up against him, both on and off the dance floor. The second she began to strip off she was reminded why she'd no business daydreaming that something could happen between them.

The ugly puckered scars criss-crossing her body had been incorporated into her colourful tattoo designs but she knew they were there and that was enough reason for her to keep herself hidden. They were a permanent reminder of what happened when she made stupid choices in life. Even though her family didn't have the same physical markings from the aftermath of the crash, the damage she'd caused was blatantly obvious. Now Talia was serious about settling down and making a home with Mum and the baby, she wasn't about to do something else stupid to spoil that like falling for a man with as much personal baggage as she had. She liked Ben and she was fond of Hugh, but she had too much going on in her life right now to commit to anything else.

She stepped into the shower and did her best to wash away all traces of these past nights together so she couldn't remember the way he'd held her, or the confident way he'd stepped up during the emergency in The Shed, where for once she hadn't been the only one expected to deal with the crisis. It didn't work.

Once she'd dried off she grabbed the clean white shirt hanging on the back of the door and hoped Ben wouldn't mind her borrowing it in the circumstances. Although it showed more leg than she was happy with, it was sufficient for her to wear as a makeshift dress until her own clothes were ready.

She threw her clothes in the machine on the quickest wash possible and took a seat on the sofa to wait.

Ben phoned for a taxi once he knew Tom was settled in Recovery, thankful Mollie had volunteered to lock up for him so he could go straight home. She'd been a great help tonight again, not afraid to get her clothes dirty when they were scrabbling about trying to keep Tom conscious and sharing some of the responsibilities Ben usually had to deal with on his own. It was good to have someone to count on in times of crisis and he was lucky to have Mollie in his life.

He just wished she'd show him a sign that she wouldn't jump ship when he was starting to rely on her being there.

He knocked lightly on the door, hoping Amy was still around to let him in. If not he was going to have to track down the building supervisor and all he wanted to do right now was collapse into bed.

After a few breath-holding seconds he heard the bolt sliding from the door and the lock turning as he was granted entry into the house. He was going to have to get a taxi to retrieve the car first thing in the morning. After he contacted Mollie, of course, to somehow recover the keys first.

'I'm sorry—' The oft-heard apology died on his lips when the door opened and he was greeted by a far different sight than the one he'd expected. Mollie, barefoot, her hair wet and loose around her shoulders and wearing one of his shirts, sucked the breath clean out of his lungs and rendered him speechless. The vision was so surreal he wondered if he hadn't fallen asleep in the taxi and this was nothing more than a fantasy born of overwork and lack of sleep.

'I brought your keys and phone over... I was covered in blood... I thought I could wash them before you got home and Hugh was here on his own...'

He was treated to the fine sight of her bare legs as she walked away muttering a rambled explanation of her appearance, the split in the side of his shirt revealing a tantalising glimpse of a pale pink cherry-blossom design disappearing up along her thigh.

'Nice tattoo,' he said, revealing exactly where his gaze had lingered. As soon as the words left his lips he regretted them as she tugged at the hem of the shirt, suddenly self-conscious. She'd done so much for him tonight and everyone around him, and making her feel uncomfortable wasn't the way he should've repaid her kindness.

'Thanks. How's Tom?' She did her best to change the focus of their conversation but Ben couldn't seem to draw his eyes away from the creamy white skin of her thigh. He knew it was probably unheard of for tattoo artists not to have some skin art of their own, but that sneak peek of the woman behind the vintage clothes and cover girl make-up only made him want to know more about the woman behind the Ice Queen misnomer.

'Only time will tell how much use he'll regain in his fingers but physio should help him with that. Hopefully there's not too much long-term damage.' Tom's arm would remain in a splint for the foreseeable future and his aftercare would be as important as the surgery Ben had just carried out.

'I'm glad you were there.' She gave a shiver and Ben knew she was contemplating what could've happened if not for their actions. Tom could easily have bled to death if they hadn't had their pizza date upstairs.

'I couldn't have done it without you.' Her response had helped cut the waiting time for Tom to be seen to and gone some way towards preventing him going into shock and suffering a worse fate than tendon damage.

'I think you'd have managed.' She flashed him a half-smile and turned away again, heading towards the still-whirring tumble drier. As she crouched down to check the time dial he was treated to another flash of that intriguing body art and he was left wondering how far it carried on up her body.

'Does it have any significance?' The bold pink flowers entwined in the cascading vine were dedicated to so much of her body they obviously held some special meaning. Mollie didn't seem the type to undertake such a commitment on a whim. A lot of time and thought, not to mention pain, had obviously gone into the design.

It took a few seconds for her to register what he was talking about, then she brushed the cotton cover aside to reveal a little more of the blossoms. 'It's supposed to represent the fragility of life.'

Ben hunched down beside her and gently traced the delicate petals with his fingertip. 'And beauty.'

Her muscles tightened beneath his exploration as his fingertips brushed over the uneven area of skin disguised by the colourful ink. The scars were deep and long enough for him to recognise the serious nature of their origin. She'd obviously gone through a lot of trauma and her body told the tale even if she'd done her best to hide it.

'I can't say I've felt very beautiful in a long time.' She rose to her feet and the curtain of his white cotton shirt fell once more to cover her thigh. Without her usual facade of make-up and bravado, standing here in all her natural beauty, she shouldn't have felt anything less than a goddess.

'You have absolutely nothing to be ashamed of. Scars are the marks of a survivor, you know that.' They both dealt on a daily basis with patients left marked for ever by their battle back from illness and injury and he was only ever humbled by their strength. Mollie was no exception.

'It doesn't make them any easier to look at in the mirror. I'm not one of your patients, Ben. I haven't been courageous or brave in the face of adversity. This is the result of a stupid decision I made when I was a kid.' Her voice tailed off into a hiccup and revealed her pain as raw as if the wounds were still open.

'Don't ever say that. You're an amazing nurse and the most compassionate person I know.' Ben stood up and forced her to look at him. He couldn't let her go on thinking she was anything other than amazing. He thought back to that morning she'd lectured Carole about looking in the mirror and learning to accept herself and it made her all the more remarkable when she was still suffering herself.

'You wouldn't say that if you knew the whole truth.' Mollie walked away and left the drier still rumbling but Ben wasn't content to let her wallow when she'd done so much for him tonight. Given what she'd already confided in him about her personal circumstances, he was only too willing to return the favour if there was anything he could do. He followed her back into the living room, unwilling to continue to let her think so badly of herself whatever had happened.

'Try me.' He doubted there was anything she could tell him now that would change his mind about the type of person she was when he'd seen it for himself these past evenings together.

'The accident cost my parents their marriage, Talia her childhood, not to mention screwed up every relationship any of us have had ever since.'

'What on earth would make you think that?'

'Dad's temper was volatile at the best of times. We spent most of our childhood getting yelled at, watching plates hit the wall if dinner hadn't been cooked and presented to his satisfaction and listening to him insult Mum about her appearance. Even though he was the one who wouldn't let her wear anything he deemed "inappropriate," including make-up. The accident stretched my parents to breaking point, splitting their time between home and the hospital with every skin graft I went through. It was my fault he couldn't handle it and walked out. Mum and Talia never got over it.'

Ben's heart broke to think of her as that traumatised child carrying all that unnecessary guilt. All he wanted to do was wrap her up and keep her safe from anyone who would ever cause her that much pain again.

'That's an awful lot of responsibility to accept for a lapse in judgement you made as a kid. We've all made mistakes in our past. That doesn't mean we should spend the rest of our lives under a cloud of guilt.' It had taken him some time to work that one out, along with the patience and understanding of his grandparents, who'd insisted he should never feel bad about imposing upon them. Eventually he'd figured out for himself he shouldn't care any more about the past than his parents did. It had been little more than an excuse for them to relinquish any parental responsibility to someone else. If it hadn't been his grandparents they would have transferred his care to foster services or a juvenile detention centre.

'My dad didn't think so. He did, however, constantly remind me of how I'd ruined my looks through sheer stupidity and was now as "hideously ugly" as my mother. He blamed me for everything and he was right when he said no one will ever want me.' Her voice was so fragile it almost shattered with the words and Ben's heart right along with it because he knew it wasn't true. He'd wanted Mollie from the first night she'd turned up at The Shed. She'd simply been conditioned to think she wasn't beautiful because her father had been on some sort of twisted power trip and now it was time for her to change the way she viewed herself.

'Because of these?' He slid his hand gently along her outer thigh, feeling every indentation of the wound that obviously still brought her so much pain. Those muscles tensed beneath him again; her shoulders shook as he dared touch her again but she didn't slap him away. It was clear then how much trust it had taken for her to let him see and feel the marks of her past. That meant more to him than any confident display of sexy flesh. He didn't care about scars or family or responsibilities when he was with Mollie because that was the only time he ever felt truly alive and free to be himself. She made the day worth getting up for and that counted for more than perceived physical perfection. In his eyes and heart she was perfect and that made her someone special, someone worth letting into his life.

'They're not the only scars I have.' Mollie swallowed hard, fighting the urge to cover up and run as she normally did when it came to this stage of a relationship. Not that she'd had many opportunities to get naked with anyone but that was her own doing, just as tonight was with Ben.

He'd seen the scars on her leg, heard the tale of how her past actions had impacted on everyone around her and he hadn't once flinched. Perhaps she wanted to test exactly how stoic he could be in the face of her ugly injuries, or for once she wanted to believe they actually didn't matter to anyone but her, but she found herself unbuttoning the shirt to show off the ugly truth.

She loosened the shirt and shrugged it down so it exposed her back but kept it clutched at the front to preserve what was left of her modesty and dignity. Her eyes closed, her lip caught between her teeth, she braced herself for the gasp or, worse, that unbearable silence while he searched for a diplomatic way to hide his revulsion. Tears brimmed on her eyelashes, waiting for the go-ahead to inevitably fall down her cheeks.

Instead, the soft pressure of Ben's lips moved slowly up her back, following the knotted trail of patched-together skin she'd decorated with colourful tattooed butterflies. She held her breath waiting to see what would happen when he reached the top of her spine, expecting at some point he'd open his eyes and see her for what she was and back away. When he slipped his arms around her waist and pulled her towards him her knees began to tremble. This was new to her and though she didn't know how to respond to the positive attention, neither did she want it to end.

His hot mouth moved ever upwards to her neck, making her shiver as he whispered, 'You're beautiful,' into her ear. She wanted to believe him. The way he held her against him, his breath ragged against her skin, made it seem possible. Even the rush of her own desire for this man was drowning out the voice in her head reeling off all the reasons she'd sworn she wouldn't do this. She slowly let go of her hold on the front of the shirt, no longer wrapped up in what would happen once he saw beyond the disguise. He already had and he was still here, still kissing her as though she were the most beautiful woman in the world.

It was easy to let herself get carried away in the fantasy where nothing else mattered except the touch of him against her skin. The buzz was so great she finally understood why her mother had such difficulty staying away from trouble.

Instead of flinching every time Ben skimmed her body with his hand, waiting for that rejection she'd become accustomed to, she savoured every brush against her sensitive flesh. The shirt bunched up by her waist as his hand rode ever higher along with her temperature, her every nerve ending on high alert as he exposed her body inch by inch to his inspection.

Her nipples tightened long before his fingers found

his way there, teasing and squeezing her breast until she almost cried out with want for him.

He darted his tongue out to tease along her neck while his fingers plucked her sensitive nub. By now it was only his sheer strength of will that was keeping her upright at all.

'I want you, Mollie.' His ragged plea was her final undoing, arousal rippling through her very core and turning her apprehension to liquid. Pressed against his hard body, she didn't doubt him for a second, nor the way her body was craving him in return.

'Not here.' Regardless of the strength of her arousal, it was never going to completely obliterate the self-doubt and paranoia. She'd never purposely held on to her virginity in some sacred vow to keep herself pure for all eternity; sex had simply never worked out for her. Until now she'd never been comfortable enough with a man to even contemplate sharing that most intimate act with him, or comfortable enough in her own skin to allow it to happen. Now at the age of thirty-one she finally felt ready, that Ben was someone she wanted to be with and for whom her body image apparently wasn't an issue. That didn't mean she was willing to let her first time happen in a frenzy on the living-room floor. It needed to be special even if she wasn't ready to admit it to Ben. In this day and age her virginity really would make her out to be some sort of freak.

'We can go to my room. Don't worry, it's at the opposite end of the apartment away from my grandfather's and there's an alarm on his door in case he gets up in the middle of the night.' He did know sufficient about her to understand her need for some privacy over whatever primal urges had already driven them to put on such a public display out here.

Ben adjusted the shirt to cover her modesty again and planted a tender kiss on her neck before he took her hand and led her down the hall. The protective way he looked after her regardless of his own substantial needs in the moment suggested to her that, whatever happened next, she was in very loving and capable hands.

Once he closed the bedroom door behind them it all became so very real. Her eyes lit on the bed dominating the room, and her mind and her pulse raced ahead to where they were going next. Perhaps she should have told him she was a virgin. He was going to find out soon anyway. It wasn't as if she could bluff her way through this any more than she could the dancing. At least then he'd known what he was getting into when he'd taken on an inexperienced, nervous partner.

For now, at least, he appeared oblivious to her lack of sophistication in the art of making love as he cupped her face in his hand and sealed her intention to see this through in one sensual, breath-stealing kiss. If he was as good a teacher in bed as he was in the dance hall it probably wouldn't be long before she was up to speed, and as he teased her lips gently apart with his tongue she stopped thinking altogether.

She fumbled with the buttons of his shirt in her desire to see the body he'd been teasing her with for so long. Just because she was a virgin it didn't mean she was averse to the temptation of a muscular masculine torso when it had been in close contact with hers on numerous occasions. Ben made quicker work of disposing of her clothing than she did with his, and she tried not to think it was because he'd had more experience in disrobing other women and rather that he couldn't wait to get her into bed.

He stilled her trembling fingers with his and gave

a slow smile as he helped her undo the last fastenings of his shirt. That simple assurance they didn't have to rush this helped her breathe a little easier, despite that self-awareness she was standing there naked and fully open to his gaze. Another soft kiss on the lips helped settle the last of her remaining nerves.

She pressed herself tightly to his body, unflinching this time as he let his hands confidently explore the gentle curve of her spine. His attraction to her wasn't in doubt as she felt the hard evidence for herself. They backed up against the edge of the bed and he eased her back onto the mattress with him. The heat consuming her body soon raged into an uncontrollable inferno, flames flaring to life so brightly with lust for this man it was possible they might just burn the house down around them.

He soon found the source of her heat, exploring her with the languid strokes of his fingertips until she was moving her body in sync with his quickening rhythm, pushing towards that final climax. She could hear herself groaning somewhere in the distance as she floated away on that wave of ecstasy as her inner muscles clenched and released with her orgasm.

Only that brief sharp pain as Ben joined her body with his brought her back down to earth. She tensed for a moment, trying to control her breathing as her body adjusted to the initial shock of having him inside her.

'Are you okay?' His voice shook with restraint but the concern in his tone promised he wouldn't make another move without affirmation. Her gasp had probably given away her inexperience as much as the tension in her body, which was slowly beginning to subside now that he'd stopped moving. That didn't mean she wanted to stop altogether.

'Uh-huh.' She nodded her head since her brain was apparently still in a post-orgasm fugue and incapable of forming actual words. That small movement alone brought a groan to his lips as their bodies rubbed together once more.

'I want this, Ben.' She said it as plainly as she could so there could be no doubt in his mind that she was ready to take the next step.

It took a few seconds for him to register what she was saying, and probably decide what he wanted to do next, then he simply whispered, 'I'll take it slow.'

He sealed his promise with another kiss to melt any residual tension in her body. She'd seen enough of this man recently to know he never said anything he didn't mean, or did anything to hurt another soul, and she believed in him to guide her safely through the unknown.

A tentative upward tilt of her hips was her signal to him that she still wanted this as much as he did.

No matter how turned on Mollie had been, there was no mistaking the tightness that had surrounded him or that sharp cry as he'd entered her. She was a virgin. Whatever reasons she had for granting him the privilege of being her first, and not telling him why, were questions for another time because now there was no going back. Especially when she was responding so enthusiastically to him.

All he could do now was ensure the experience was as good for her as he knew it would be for him. He'd considered himself fortunate to even be with this beautiful woman when she was clearly so hung up on her body issues, but for her to trust him with the most precious part of her womanhood was a responsibility he wouldn't take lightly. It was a commitment he hadn't anticipated making, but they'd shared so much over the course of these past days he couldn't imagine walking away from her even if she had told him she was a virgin.

It all came down to the fact he wanted to be with her. Mollie had given him so much, made him feel more wanted and appreciated than he had in an age. He'd spent so long on a relationship that was never going to work, with a woman who wanted him to be less than he was, it would've been an act of self-sabotage not to pursue this connection he had with Mollie. She was someone willing to make as many sacrifices in the name of love as he was. It was obvious that was what this was—love—she would never have given herself to him otherwise, and, though it was a sobering thought and further complication in his life, it was a relief to finally give a name to the demon plaguing his every waking moment, too. He was in love with Mollie and the realisation only fuelled his desire for her.

They moved together slowly, as in tune as they had been since the moment she'd walked into his personal life. He didn't see her scars any more than she seemed to recognise his flaws. Not everyone could put up with his busy lifestyle and perhaps he did spread himself too thinly, but Mollie accepted that was just who he was and didn't put any pressure on him to change. It only made him want to be with her more. To love her more.

Every stroke claimed another part of his soul as hers; that emotional attachment between them growing as deep as the well of trust he saw reflected in her eyes. Their lives now were so deeply entwined he could no longer see a way to separate them. Nor did he want to. Not when he'd finally found his peace.

Mollie's breath came in small erotic groans, her head thrown back in abandon to the motion of their bodies as his sole pursuit became her all-encompassing pleasure. He kissed and licked all those areas he already knew were sensitive while he drove into her molten core until those groans of pleasure became cries of complete fulfilment ringing in the night. As she fully opened up beneath him, that current of desire carried him right along with her.

Mollie needed time to catch her breath and come to terms with what had just happened. Tonight changed everything for her and not only because of the physical barriers Ben had helped her to overcome. Simply being able to share her body with him without fear of ridicule was a game changer for her. That confidence booster was a step ever closer to that new, independent life she'd imagined lost to her. The trouble was she couldn't imagine sharing herself with anyone other than Ben now.

'Why didn't you tell me?' he said softly beside her.

She closed her eyes, unable to meet his gaze even after everything they'd shared because that information she'd held back was something she should have prewarned him about.

'You have a certain reputation yourself, Mr Sheridan. Would you really have wanted to take on an inexperienced spinster who lives with her mum when I'm sure you have the pick of the entire female species at your beck and call?' Suddenly she felt very vulnerable lying there naked in his bed, comparing herself to all those who'd probably lain there before her. She tried to pull the covers from the bed up over herself in a late attempt to hide her insecurities, but Ben pushed them away again and let his hand skim over her body instead.

'I'll admit there've been women in my life since Penny.'

She stiffened.

'But…things never went further than a date. You know reputations are an exaggeration of the truth. There hasn't been anyone I wanted to let into my life, into my bed, until now. It's taken me a long time to trust again. That's why I know this was a big deal to you, too. You've given me so much tonight and if I'd known… well, I could've made things better for you.' He slid his hand gently up her spine and this time the shivers he created came from anticipation rather than fear. Every time he touched her now those new heights of pleasure he'd helped her discover would come back in a rush of hormones and sensations.

'It gets better?' She couldn't help but tease him, knowing he would most definitely rise to the occasion. There was no way of knowing if tonight would be a one-off and, if so, she didn't want it to end.

'Do I need to show you?' He was grinning now as he continued his perusal of her curves with his fingers, grazing over every erogenous zone and driving her to distraction.

'Maybe…' All pretence of coyness vanished then as he moved between her thighs, testing her readiness with his fingers until she no longer cared about anything other than exploring every new facet of her womanhood with this man.

CHAPTER SEVEN

'HOW ARE YOU this morning?' Ben's now oh-so-familiar hands slid around Mollie's waist as she stood at the breakfast bar in his kitchen pouring two glasses of pure orange juice. She was wearing his shirt again to cover the modesty she'd long forgotten last night, along with her clothes in the tumble drier, while he was padding around the apartment in nothing more than a pair of boxer shorts and a smile. To her there seemed no more intimate picture than the two of them together sharing breakfast and the sunrise. Well, perhaps one other thing but she'd made sure they did that behind closed doors.

'Thirsty.' She handed him a glass, pretty sure he was in dire need of refreshments too after his exertions. They'd worked up quite a sweat in the joint exploration of her sexuality last night and this morning. She knew there'd be a thousand and one questions for her when she did the walk of shame home in yesterday's clothes but none of that had mattered to her during the course of her time with Ben. Even this morning, when her absence would be more noticeable than ever, she wasn't in any hurry to leave. She didn't want this moment to end.

Spending the night with him had opened her eyes to a whole new world awaiting her—a love life—and she was keen to catch up on all the years she'd missed out on. She didn't know if it was supposed to be like this every time but sex with Ben was something special, every second of which she intended to relish, and she would be more than happy to spend the rest of the day back in bed with him.

During her nursing years she'd always been a keen learner and this was no different. She wanted him to show her, to teach her everything there was to know about his body, and her own. He'd brought her to such heights of pleasure she hadn't known she was capable of reaching and that alone was intoxicating enough, even without being madly in love with him. It wasn't something she knew a lot about other than it drove the women in her life a little crazy and now she could see why. It was difficult to think straight, or about anything other than being with him, and after last night she doubted she ever would again.

Ben knocked back the glass of orange in one shot, the sight of him standing there with his abs on show, condensation from the glass dripping down his chest, like watching a real-life diet soda commercial. There was no way fruit juice was ever going to be enough to quench her dry mouth now, but she did hope it would go some way to replenish her energy levels so she could test him on whether his prowess and her thrall with him had been more than mere naivety.

They both slammed their glasses down on the counter at the same time before launching at each other in a frenzy of desire. She didn't care about the granite worktop biting against her skin as he slammed her up against it with the full weight of his body when his lips were locked around hers, focusing all of her nerve endings in one place. He cupped her backside in his hands in an act of such possession she literally went weak at the knees. She knew she was his, body and soul, when she ached for him so badly.

'What the hell are you doing in my house?' The angry voice of Ben's grandfather followed by the tight grip of his fingers around her wrist yanked Mollie out of her loved-up haze.

Her eyes fluttered open to see pyjama-clad Hugh, red-faced and only millimetres from her face. In a matter of seconds she'd gone from blissfully happy to confused and afraid, but Ben was there providing a safety barrier between them and trying to gently pry his grandfather's hand from her arm.

'Grandad? Grandad? This is Mollie, remember?' Ben used that same level tone she'd heard him use with patients, even though this was very much a personal matter that had startled them both out of their reverie.

It had been easy to forget the complications of carrying on a relationship when his grandfather was in residence and clearly easily confused. She could only imagine what was going on in his head now to find her and Ben together in such a compromising position.

Spit formed at the corner of his thin lips as he confronted them and, though Mollie felt sorry for him and Ben that he no longer even seemed to recognise his own grandson in his current state, she had her own issues to deal with. That display of aggression couldn't fail to create flashbacks of her father unleashing his rage on the family, and even though Mollie hadn't had it physically directed at her the fear was all the same. There was no way she would ever put herself in a position to be that cowering victim again, and Hugh's outburst showed her just how much hurt she was potentially opening herself up to by getting involved here.

She thought about denying what he was saying, or

even trying to reason with him, but she was paralysed with the fear of saying or doing the wrong thing and antagonising him further.

'I'm your grandson, Ben. This is my place. Remember? We had to sell your house after Gran passed away and you couldn't manage on your own.' Ben was left with no other choice but to cruelly spell out the facts and she knew every word must have broken his heart to say. How often he'd had to repeat them didn't bear thinking about.

'We were so happy.' Hugh broke down in tears and let go of her arm to hold his head in his hands. She found an inner strength to back away towards the door as Ben went to comfort his grandfather.

'I should go,' she mouthed, and she grabbed the clothes Ben had thoughtfully taken out of the drier and left neatly folded on the kitchen table for her. As she watched him gather his grandfather in a hug and let him cry on his shoulder, she knew there was no room for her here.

Ben knocked on Mollie's office door, his heart pounding with the uncertainty of how she'd react to this morning's events or even seeing him here. He hated the feeling of powerlessness watching his grandfather succumb to this cruel illness just as much as having to watch Mollie walk out of the apartment without giving chase. That great strain on his loyalties was the very reason he should've known better than to get involved with another woman so he didn't blame her for not wanting to stick around. Few people did in the circumstances. Even a night of fantastic sex couldn't counteract the effect of an elderly man with dementia on the scene.

No matter how much he'd wanted to apologise to her

for what had happened and hug her, too, his grandfather had had to come first this morning when it had been clear he was in such a bad way. Ben would never have contemplated having her to stay over if his grandfather had shown previous signs of aggression and put her in any sort of danger.

He'd never displayed that level of temper before, not even in Ben's younger days when he'd had difficulty staying out of trouble. He wasn't convinced the *real* Hugh Sheridan would've acted like that and it brought a new problem they were going to have to face together. That failure to recognise his own family member had left Ben no other choice but to seek immediate medical help to stabilise his mood.

The bonus of being in the profession was access to those who were able to offer his grandfather the best treatment available without joining the ever-growing waiting lists. Not everyone had that option and he was grateful they'd been able to be seen straight away. Unfortunately it had meant abandoning Mollie at a time when he should've been there for her, too.

He didn't hesitate to enter her room when she called out her customary cheery invitation to enter.

Her smile faltered a little when he strode into the room as though he deserved her time and his bravado did threaten to desert him there and then but she was too important to him to simply accept defeat.

'I'm so sorry, Mollie. I know you must be mad at me, but he wasn't in his right mind this morning. I couldn't leave him.' He crouched down on the floor beside her chair and took her hand in his, begging for her to see how difficult the decision had been for him to make and how his conscience was continually battling to ensure he did the right thing.

'I know. Is he all right? Are you?' She stroked the side of his face with her hand and immediately quietened the chaos going on in Ben's head. She understood him and the decisions he was forced to make more than anyone else ever had, even though they'd really only known each other for a short while. Even now, when she had every right to take offence at the treatment she'd received at the hands of him and his grandfather this morning, her concern remained solely for their welfare. That said a lot about the kind of person she was and how infrequently she put her own feelings first and only served to increase the weight of guilt on his shoulders.

He knew something of the sacrifices she already made for her own family and he didn't want to be another burden upon her good nature.

'We're fine. He settled down eventually and Amy's keeping an eye on him until I get back. She assures me she's seen all this before and it's part and parcel of caring for dementia patients. I'm sorry if either of us hurt you this morning. I just wanted to come and make sure you were okay. I will totally understand if…if you don't want to see me again. Don't feel obligated because of the contest. I can always withdraw our names and give a donation instead.'

If there'd been any doubt in her mind about what she was getting herself into, this morning's events had spelled it out clearly for her and it wouldn't come as any great surprise if she'd decided enough was enough. That didn't mean he had to like it.

Every time he thought of his grandfather's tight grip on her arm and that look of fear on her face he wanted to smash something in pure rage. If it had been any other man in any other circumstances he probably would have but it wasn't going to help matters at the minute. From the little information she'd shared about her father's cruel nature, and his grandfather's behaviour towards her this morning, she'd been a victim of enough male aggression to last a lifetime.

'Is that what you want?' A frown dimpled her forehead as she contemplated what it was he was saying to her.

As much as it was killing him, he was giving her the option of backing away now before things got even more complicated, and painful, for either of them. He didn't have any magic cure for dementia or a solution to the demands it would create on a relationship, but he could hope Mollie could see as much potential they had as a couple as he did. He really didn't think he'd recover if she left him when she was the one person who truly seemed to care for him.

'No, but I don't want to hurt you. I'm always going to have to prioritise Grandad's health over my love life.' She'd already shown her trust in him and an emotional investment that went beyond the realms of a mere one-night stand and it didn't seem fair that he had nothing to offer her in return.

'I'm a nurse and I'm used to dealing with the elderly and infirm. I don't take it personally.'

'You don't have to downplay it for my sake. Last night was a huge step and this morning, well, I'm sure it wasn't how you imagined the morning after your first time.' He wasn't trying to be big-headed; everyone remembered their first time and not always with fondness. He'd wanted to make it special for her, and being attacked by his grandfather and practically shoved out of the door next morning wasn't the memory he wanted her to take away from their night together. Given another chance, he would have done things differently. Say in a secluded hotel room with a do-not-disturb sign on the door.

She'd given a lot of herself to him, more than he'd realised at the time, and giving him her virginity wasn't something she would've done without a lot of soul-searching. He didn't know what he'd done to deserve such an honour but he hoped she wasn't regretting it in the cold light of day. Life was so terribly complicated right now he didn't know what the future held for any of them, but he did know he didn't want to let her go. If it wasn't too late he wanted the chance to prove how much she meant to him even if his actions, or apparent lack of them, this morning had made her believe otherwise.

'Just because we had sex doesn't mean I'm expecting a marriage proposal.' She pushed the chair away, wheeling across the floor so she had some space from him and letting that mask slip. No matter how hard she protested otherwise, she had been hurt or else she wouldn't have been so defensive now.

'That's exactly why I'm asking you if you want to back out now. I love being with you, Mollie, but not if it comes at the expense of your happiness.' He got up from his begging position but he didn't follow her across the room, not wanting to crowd her, so she could decide what it was she wanted, holding his breath because he desperately wanted it to be him.

'Perhaps we should cool things down. We have rushed into this—'

Ben's lungs deflated along with that last hope. 'That's what I thought.'

'I signed the rental agreement for my own flat today. I've finally got the freedom I wanted. There's a lot going on in both of our lives at the minute. Why don't we just concentrate on the dancing for now?'

'We can do that.' The words stuck in his throat as he took a direct blow where it hurt the most—his heart.

He'd never tried to fool himself into thinking one night with him could have turned her from virgin ice queen into a vixen with an insatiable sexual appetite, who would welcome him into her bed at any personal cost, but he was more crushed by her rejection than he had ever been by Penny's. Probably because Mollie had seemed much more accepting of his set-up at home. And because he loved her. He guessed everyone had their limits and she'd reached hers in the kitchen this morning.

Given the choice of still spending time with her at rehearsals or not at all was a no-brainer even if it meant the agony of having her in his arms without actually *being* with her any more.

From that first impulsive kiss he'd known there'd be heartbreak somewhere along the way. He just hadn't realised it would be his.

'Shouldn't lover boy be helping you with the heavy lifting?' Talia had been relegated to a supervisory role since Mollie refused to let her carry any of the removal crates. She'd only let her pregnant sister help with the move at all because she was the one with the driving licence and the friend willing to lend her his van to move Mollie's few possessions across the city into her new flat.

It wouldn't have been fair to ask Ben for assistance when she'd insisted she needed some space. Hugh's actions that morning had shaken her to her core and made her question what it was she was getting herself into, and when Ben had pushed her to make a decision her instinct had been to protect herself and take a step back. She couldn't afford to invite him back in her life when it had devastated her to let him go in the first place.

It wasn't going to be easy to simply turn her back on Ben and forget what they'd shared together. Not least because she was determined to see this dance competition through to the end, because when all of this was over she was still going to have to work with him. Perhaps it only hurt so much because he had been her first, but for once she was going to follow the example set by the womenfolk in her family in regards to what not to do in relationships and make sure she was the one setting the rules.

'I told you, we're not *together* together.' Her absence the other night hadn't gone unnoticed and, though she'd had to confess something had gone on with Ben, she'd tried to downplay what had happened. There was no point in pretending it could be anything more than a one-off when the circumstances wouldn't allow it to take root and blossom into anything more significant.

Ironically, spending the night in Ben's apartment, as life-changing for her as it had been, had also given her the impetus to take her future into her own hands and make that final decision on moving out.

There'd been a mixed reaction to her bid for independence from home. It had taken Talia's baby news to soften the blow for her mother. Once she'd realised there wasn't going to be an empty space in her life, it had seemed to galvanise her into action for the first time in ages. She even seemed keen to help Mollie pack as she made plans for redecorating her bedroom and transforming it into a nursery. Perhaps she'd make a better grandmother than she'd ever been as a mother with that chance to start the family over again with a clean slate. Mollie couldn't help but wonder as they accepted their separation from each other so readily if they hadn't been enabling each other into this rut over these past years. This could be the new start they all needed.

The flat wasn't spacious or particularly glamorous but it was close to her work, distant enough from her family to give her that sense of freedom without being too far to check in every now and then, and had everything she needed to be comfortable. It was hers.

'I know you, Mollie, and, mark my words, this will end in tears.' Despite being told specifically not to open any boxes, Talia was already ripping open those marked for the kitchen and unpacking the dishes.

'You're managing to cope without a significant other permanently in your life so I don't see why it should be any different for me.' Mollie wasn't about to take advice from her pregnant single sister, who was determined to do it all alone. At least they had their stubborn streak in common, if not much else.

'Don't you think if I could go back and change things I would? This is exactly why I'm trying to prevent you from making the same mistakes I did.' There was such a profound sadness in the way Talia stroked her hand over her budding baby belly, it suggested she'd had a closer bond with the father than she'd ever been prepared to admit to. So far the only information she'd given on his identity was that she'd met him abroad and it had been a hot and heavy affair with no chance of surviving beyond a holiday romance. She wouldn't even be drawn as far as to name the man responsible for getting her pregnant, and, Mollie suspected, breaking her heart.

'I appreciate that, I really do, but I have no intention of getting into something I can't handle. I'm the sensible one, remember?' It was nice to have that level of concern from a loved one about her well-being, but she'd already found enough inner strength to take a step back from everybody's personal lives to focus on her own. That included Ben's and Hugh's.

She was forced to dodge the balled-up newspaper Talia threw at her head at the suggestion she was the nonsensible one of the pair, even though they both knew it to be true. Mollie hoped that since she'd opened up her heart and let Ben in, for however short a time, it wouldn't change that dynamic.

CHAPTER EIGHT

'I KNOW YOU'RE bound to be nervous, Shirley, but you've already come through so much and you know you're in the best hands with Mr Sheridan.' Mollie liked to check in with her patients before and after surgery to put them at ease. They saw so many different doctors and consultants from the point of diagnosis it was important that some continuity of care was in place. Having a familiar face at all stages of treatment provided some sense of security in such a time of upheaval.

'Oh, yes. He's such a nice man and he did such a good job on my breast reconstruction I have every faith he can make me a nipple that looks as good as the real thing. I'll just be glad when it's all over.'

'It won't be long. Then you can treat yourself to a whole new wardrobe for your cruise.' Mollie reminded her of the trip she'd been planning for weeks so she had something positive to focus on before she was wheeled into Theatre.

'My youngest daughter's taking me shopping so you can bet your life I'll be taking a suitcase full of summer dresses and swimsuits on board that ship.'

'Good. You deserve it.' It always aided a faster recovery when patients had something to look forward to at the end of their gruelling journey. Even better when they had enough confidence in their body to show it off again.

'I hope you're saving me that sun lounger by the pool you promised.' Ben approached Shirley's bedside dressed in his scrubs and a smile that had surely melted the heart of every woman he'd walked past. Mollie included.

'Right beside mine. I'll be sure to pick you up a pair of swim shorts when I'm out shopping, too.' Shirley's jovial banter with Ben made it obvious they'd got to know each other pretty well since she'd been transferred into his care. It wasn't often busy surgeons had the time to spend with patients outside sharing information about the procedures they were performing. This little insight into the extra mile he went to in getting to know the people he was operating on and earning their trust wasn't helping Mollie to get her feelings for him back on a neutral level.

'Well, we'll get you through this surgery first, then we're all set. I just wanted to check that you're clear on what's going to happen in Theatre today.' Ben seamlessly slipped back into his surgeon persona, but coming here to chat pre-op would undoubtedly make his patient more relaxed than she would've been handing over control of her body to a complete stranger.

With that level of empathy it was no wonder he found it so difficult to prioritise his own wants and needs above his grandfather's. It also made Mollie hang her head in shame that she hadn't been able to do the same for Hugh.

Shirley nodded and turned to Mollie. 'Will you be in there with me?'

'No, I don't—'

'You're welcome to assist, if you'd like.' Ben shrugged,

showing no sign of the same turmoil that was raging inside her simply from being in close proximity to him. She might have called time on their relationship before it had fully formed, but it didn't mean her attraction to him or her feelings for him had diminished in the interim.

There were a lot of personal reasons why she should decline and duck out of the offer to spend more time with him, but on a professional level she knew it would benefit her patient and provide her with a unique learning experience. This kind of opportunity would give her more insight into what these women went through and what the procedures involved. Ultimately it would help her relate to her patients and that had to come before her own discomfort.

'Sure,' she said as brightly as she could muster, ignoring the slight smirk she was sure she saw tugging at Ben's mouth.

Nipple reconstruction was a procedure Ben frequently carried out but there seemed to be so much more on the line with Mollie in the theatre with him. Not only was she seeing him at work, but Shirley's request for her to be there was forcing them to spend time together when he knew she would probably have tried to avoid him for as long as possible.

He understood why Mollie had backed away, that was why he'd given her an out, but he had been hoping she saw something in him that Penny hadn't. That she'd thought him worth taking a chance on. Deep down he was still hoping she was different and he could convince her they could be good for one another. Mollie had certainly made him re-evaluate his situation and see that there was still a place in it for him to have a life of his own. Preferably with her in it. He'd believed he was doing the same for her but that one setback with his grandfather had prompted her inner ice queen to freeze him out again. If he could simply find a way to reconnect with her he might be able to get them back on course again. Mollie had given him a glimpse of the future he could've had and without her he didn't have anything to look forward to any more.

For now he was concentrating on giving Shirley her life back and praying karma was keeping score.

Once the area was marked and numb from the anaesthetic, Ben began to make his incision.

'We make a bow-tie flap with the skin on the breast, making sure that's symmetrical as possible with the opposite breast. Tuck the sides under, including a small amount of fat to bulk out the nipple, and attach the sides end to end.' He talked Mollie through each stage and let her see everything he was doing before he moved on to the next step.

She was watching him intently, taking everything in, and he knew this training would help her prepare her future patients as well as she could now she knew exactly what the reconstruction entailed.

'Sometimes it's possible to take part of the nipple from the remaining breast and attach it to the new breast in a nipple-sharing graft. As I've discussed with Shirley, it wasn't possible in this case.' He pulled the flaps of skin together to form the little nub that was more for aesthetic and psychological purposes than function, and Mollie dabbed around the area with cotton to keep it clean.

'Then we close the raw area where we've borrowed the skin.' He let silence dominate the operating room while he made sure all incisions were closed with sutures, and left the final step of dressing the wound to Mollie.

It was her job for the first few weeks to monitor and change these dressings in the outpatient clinic to make sure they remained dry and in place to maximise the chances of success. As with any surgery there were always risks but bruising, swelling and infection were thankfully infrequent complications.

'And then, when the wound is healed, it's over to you to add the finishing touches with your tattooing skills.' He would never underestimate the part she played in the process. Not only did she add that final touch of realism, which counted for so much towards helping their patients feel *normal* again, but she was also the point of contact for any problems or concerns post-care. Although she mightn't realise it, she shouldered a lot of responsibility for each person who came through the clinic doors.

'We make quite the team,' she conceded as they prepped Shirley for her return to the ward so she could recover.

'Yes. Yes, we do.' Ben held eye contact with her, trying to make her see that was exactly why she should believe they could make it as a couple in their own right, supporting each other and working together to achieve their mutual goals.

He saw her throat bob as she swallowed and looked away, making it obvious there were still feelings there for him whether or not she wanted to admit it.

'I need to go and scrub out.' She practically ran out, stripping off her protective clothing as she went, but Ben wouldn't be put off so easily and waited for her back on the ward.

'What are we going to do about dance rehearsals? We might be a team but that doesn't mean we don't have to work at it.'

'I won't be finished until late, I'm afraid. I've a lot of paperwork to catch up on now.' She didn't even attempt to slow down to speak to him and Ben ended up trailing her back to her office. The empty waiting room and absence of staff made it clear the clinic had ended for the day even if Mollie hadn't.

'We could do it here.' He barged on into her office, regardless of her attempt to close the door in his face.

'Pardon?' Her cheeks were flushed as she turned to face him and gave away what direction her wayward thoughts had just taken.

Ben couldn't help but laugh. She would never be so flustered if he wasn't still having some effect on her. 'Dance rehearsal? There's plenty of room in here if we move a few things around.'

'Oh. Right. Yeah. I knew that. I'm not sure it's really appropriate, though…'

'Why not? Everyone knows we're taking part and we have the hospital's backing, after all.' He began rearranging the furniture, pushing chairs and trolleys to one side so they had a wide enough space to make their turns without banging into anything.

'I suppose I do need the practice, but what about our music?'

Ben pulled his phone from his pocket. 'Ta-da! Thanks to the wonders of technology I already have it downloaded. Any more excuses or can we get started?'

'I guess.' She rolled her eyes and stepped towards him with all the anxiety and nervousness she'd displayed on that first night. They'd come a long way since then and he wanted to remind her of that.

He took her in hold but she seemed determined to keep an invisible wall between them, standing as far back from him as she could. The music started and Ben pulled her to him so they actually looked and felt like a couple rather than two strangers forced into an awkward dance at a wedding.

They started off with the steps he'd already showed her, but they had the small matter of a dance contest to contend with so he talked her through the foot position required for a smooth promenade. Mollie was quick to pick up the steps and it wasn't long before they fell back into that easy rhythm, moving together as one. The rise and fall of their bodies in perfect harmony and her soft breath on his face couldn't fail to remind him of the night they'd spent together. As he looked into Mollie's desire-darkened eyes he knew she felt it, too.

It was impossible to watch Ben work and not be impressed by his level of skill and compassion. She was trying not to let it cloud her judgement or the decisions she'd made to try and protect her from making the same mistakes her mother had made over again. Impossible now that she was flush against his chest, their layers of clothes the only difference from the last time they'd had physical contact.

His heart was beating the same rapid tempo as hers, so out of time even with the moderately quick pace of the dance. She was lost in his eyes, her feet moving independently of the rest of her body and carrying her wherever he needed her to be. When they were dancing it was easy to believe there was nothing on this earth that could stop them from being together.

The music stopped but they didn't break apart, neither apparently willing for the spell to be broken or to let reality creep back in between them. That magnetic pull was drawing her back to him, close enough that she could feel his breath on her lips. She closed her eyes, wanting to give herself over to that sensual bliss of a tender kiss, but that sensible Mollie wasn't going to be so easily subdued and projected images into her mind of Hugh's fingers digging into her wrist, the flash of temper she'd seen once in Ben. That was all it took to save her from repeating her mistake.

'Dance lesson over. I really need to catch up on my work.' Her trembling voice betrayed the strength of her rejection as she pushed him away, but she needed him to go so she had space to wail and cry over everything she was throwing away in peace.

'We still have the turns to work on.' Ben was every bit as shaky as she was but still he pushed for more.

'Can we do it tomorrow night? Please, Ben.' It was a desperate plea for him to heed her decision to stop this in its tracks, even when it seemed she was having trouble following her own advice.

He gave a silent nod and reached for the door handle. A final act of kindness when she was at breaking point and one more heat-filled gaze or brush of his skin against hers would either result in her tearing off his clothes or dissolving into a puddle of tears. She couldn't be sure which way the pendulum would swing if she gave into her emotions once and for all.

When the door slammed shut behind him only the weeping option remained.

It was a couple of days before Ben contacted Mollie again. He knew he'd pushed her too far and he was fighting a losing battle. She'd made her decision and he had to accept that she didn't want a relationship with him or lose her altogether. They still had to get through this dance competition, but after their last rehearsal he knew it was going to be a tough call trying to get her back to The Shed. In the end he'd had to play dirty and remind her she'd volunteered to paint a mural for them, and with Tom out of action all of the volunteers had to put in extra shifts to try and get the place spruced up. If he could at least get her there, let her see he wasn't going to put her under pressure to get back on track as a couple, he might be able to persuade her to rehearse again.

She was waiting for him outside The Shed, paint supplies in hand, and she seemed to stand up straighter when she saw him coming. As though she was steeling herself to go into battle. After everything they'd shared and the hopes he'd had that they could still salvage their relationship, he wasn't ashamed to admit it hurt. Not that he would let her see that when he was doing his best to coax her back into a non-threatening dance partnership.

'Hey. Thanks for coming.' He left the shutters down so they could have some privacy but opened the door and flicked all the lights on so she could see for herself that work still needed to be done to get the place ready for any future visitors.

'I didn't want to break my promise and let anyone down.' She got straight to work unpacking her materials and giving a clear signal she was only here to work and fulfil the duties she'd promised to carry out before things had become complicated.

'I appreciate it.'

'So, what would you like me to paint?'

The wall was a blank canvas and Ben knew whatever she added to it would improve it one hundred per cent. It would also make him think of her every time he came into the room. He wasn't sure that was going to be conducive to forgetting her once the contest was over and there were no more excuses to see her outside work.

'Anything you like. What about some cherry blossoms?' He couldn't help himself from teasing but only succeeded in prompting her into giving him the death stare.

'Behave yourself or you can do it yourself. I believe you're quite handy with a can of spray paint.' The burn didn't sting nearly as much as it should when the person inflicting it was smiling and looking pretty smug with herself.

That teasing about his past misdemeanours helped ease some of the tension between them and would hopefully pave the way for another foray into the world of ballroom dancing before the contest was upon them.

Even if Ben hadn't been in contact with her, Mollie knew she'd have had trouble staying away. Her fevered dreams of dances and kisses were making him impossible to forget. Their last encounter had made her question if those kisses might be worth taking a risk after all.

She painted the outline of a woodland scene and set Ben to task colouring the blades of grass in the hope it would occupy his mind and keep him from making any further innuendo referencing the intimacy they'd shared only nights ago.

'I think I'm getting repetitive strain injury,' he complained eventually and downed his paintbrush in his restlessness.

'Well, we can't have you suing me if I'm putting your livelihood at risk. We can finish this another time.' Mollie began to clean her brushes and pack up her paints. She could store them here until the job was complete. It wouldn't take long and there was nothing stopping her from popping in on her days off. When Ben wasn't here to distract her.

'We just need a break.' Ben walked over to the shelves at the back of the room and turned on the radio, filling the airwaves with the sounds of nineties' pop songs.

It brought back memories of the summer Talia had spent teaching her cheesy dance routines, which were a world away from the grace and passion of her lessons with Ben.

'May I have this dance?' He made a sweeping bow before her as he made his proposal.

'We can't dance to this.' Mollie laughed at the absurdity of the notion the steps he'd taught her could be related in any way to the repetitive squawking going on in the background.

'Why not? There's no law saying we're limited to only performing a waltz. You can still dance for fun, you know.' His eyes were sparkling with mischief as he took her hand and offered her some respite from the usual staid rules of ballroom. He didn't give her a chance to refuse even if his naughty disregard for convention wasn't infectious.

This was an altogether different arrangement than she was used to as he whirled her into what she could only describe as a jive of some sort. They were practically bouncing across the floor as Ben spun her in and out of his hold until she was dizzy. These were the moments she found it difficult to let go, when the two of them were laughing and carefree and totally enamoured with each other.

When the song ended and gave way to adverts they were left with their arms wrapped around each other, panting from their exertions. Mollie smiled up at him, trying to catch her breath again but reluctant to leave go of him again. He obviously took it as a sign she was willing to ditch her vow as he dipped his head and tried to kiss her.

'No.' She turned her head to dodge his lips when she knew her resolve was weakening by the second.

'Why not, Mollie? You know we both want this. We're good together. We deserve some happiness for ourselves.' He made all valid points.

'I don't want to get hurt again, Ben, and I don't see how we can possibly have a future.'

'If you keep focusing on what could happen instead of the possibilities you have in front of you you're never going to find peace. Why can't we just seize what we have in this moment and enjoy it for what it is?'

For him that probably meant a passionate fling when she'd made it clear she didn't want anything more serious. The trouble was, kissing or no kissing, every minute she spent with Ben she knew she was falling deeper in love with him and she'd sold her soul piece by piece in exchange for their snatched time together. There was no reason left for her to hold back when her fate was already sealed.

She pulled his head down towards her and kissed him, hard and fast and eager to catch up on everything she'd been missing.

Ben latched onto her as though she were the very air he needed to breathe, their bodies crashing against the shelves as they found each other again. Her skin prickled with the heat from the flames of their passion and she didn't protest as Ben tore at her clothes, exposing her to his gaze, his mouth and the cool night air.

She didn't want time to think; there'd been too much of that lately and tonight all she wanted to do was act on those instincts telling her to love Ben in whatever way she could. His body was hard against hers, pressing his need so insistently where she wanted him most. With trembling hands, she undid his fly, eliciting a sharp gasp from him that made her bolder still. She pushed aside the layers of fabric to claim her prize, grabbing his erection and making her intentions known beyond doubt. This time she was no timid virgin who needed to be treated with kid gloves; she was a red-blooded woman fired with passion who knew exactly what she wanted.

Her scars were barely of any consequence to her as she stripped away the remainder of her own clothes to accept him. Ben had seen them for himself, heard the stories behind them and he was still crazed with lust for her.

He hooked her leg around his waist, braced the two of them against the shelving and thrust inside her, immediately satisfying that aching need he'd awakened in her since the first time he'd kissed her.

She was forced to grab hold of the shelf above her head for support, praying it was secure enough for both of them as Ben drove deep time and time again until they'd both satisfied their basest needs. Their climactic cries drowned out the white noise of the radio along with any doubts they should be together.

CHAPTER NINE

WORK AND THE trials of his grandfather aside, these past days had been the best of Ben's life. He and Mollie had spent whatever time they could find together practising their dance routine and making love. Neither of them knew what the future held but for now they were content with what they had.

He'd looked into putting a personal care package together for his grandfather that would help them all live as normal a life as possible. So far it hadn't been possible to stay over with Mollie, but tonight he was taking steps to address that. They'd decided on dinner at her place and Ben was hoping they might actually get to spend a whole night alone.

'I'm off out, Grandad. I've left my number in case anyone needs to get hold of me.'

'Are you seeing Mollie? She's a nice girl. Reminds me a lot of my Ellen.' In a rare moment of lucidity his grandfather remembered who she was, but having him bring her up in conversation now as Ben was going out of the door to meet her was something of a surprise and proved he was on the ball enough in those brief intervals to read his grandson's mood. There was always more of a spring to Ben's step on those nights he knew he was going to see Mollie.

'Yeah…er… I like spending time with her. I hope that's okay?'

His grandfather gripped him firmly by the shoulder.

'You go for it, son. She's special. Don't ever let me get in the way of you living your life. All your gran and I ever wanted was for you to be happy.' Tears welled in his eyes as he willed Ben to leave him behind in the pursuit of his own soul mate. They'd never discussed the idea of moving him into more permanent care because it wasn't an option Ben had ever wanted to consider. Now Hugh was basically telling him he didn't want to be that burden holding his grandson back from anything that would bring him joy. It was a lot to take in when Ben had always believed that final decision rested on his shoulders and no one else's.

'Thanks, Grandad.' Ben pulled him into a back-slapping bear hug, choking back his own tears. To have his blessing on the relationship and relieving him of some of that responsibility of his care when the time came when he could no longer cope with him at home meant everything. Now all he had to do was convince Mollie they could have a future after all.

Mollie had cleaned the apartment to within an inch of its life, showered, put on the sexy underwear she'd purchased with Ben in mind and was waiting for him to arrive.

There was no reason to be nervous, yet she couldn't bring herself to order the dinner she'd promised him when the anticipation of their night together had been fuel enough to get her through the day. She'd wait until they'd worked up an appetite before they put in the call for more sustenance. He'd promised her a full night together with the assurance it wasn't for any other reason than for them to enjoy each other's company without interruption.

Even though she was expecting the rap on the door her heart gave an extra beat when Ben confirmed his arrival with a loud knock. He looked hot as hell, too, standing there on her doorstep with carnal intention written all over his handsome face. It wouldn't have mattered if he'd turned up wearing his scrubs, a tux or nothing but a smile because they both knew the reason he was there and it wasn't to practise their dance steps.

'Did someone order a booty call?' He leaned against the door frame with the lazy sort of smile that would make aphrodisiacs a billion-dollar industry if they could bottle it.

'Sorry. I think you've been prank called. We get a lot of that around here. I had five pizza-delivery boys sent here last week.' She feigned nonchalance even though there was every chance she would drop into a dead faint at the sight of him at any given second.

'Oh? I sincerely hope they didn't get the kind of welcome I'm expecting.' His lips were on hers before she had a chance to make another sassy comeback as he pushed into the flat and kicked the door shut behind him.

With her arms and legs wrapped around him, he carried her easily with him across the floor.

'The bedroom's behind you,' she mumbled, the compact nature of her new abode and the proximity of the rooms at least proving useful on this occasion. They wouldn't have to wait too long to be properly reunited.

'Good.' The growl of his impatience at her ear rippled through every erogenous zone in her body until she practically fell onto the bed in surrender to her libido. There was a new depth to the urgency of his desire to match her own tonight. Hers was fuelled by the strength of her feelings for him, which she couldn't dare voice. Admitting she was in love with someone who didn't feel the same way and sticking around was tantamount to self-abuse and that was before she even added his grandfather into the equation.

Ben paused briefly to admire her lacy lingerie before unceremoniously tossing it onto the floor and she stopped thinking about everyone else other than the man she loved.

'I love you, Mollie.' The words slipped out as they lay in the afterglow of their lovemaking and Ben couldn't take them back even if he wanted to. The truth was he wanted this to work, he wanted to have a proper relationship with her and still carry on caring for his grandfather. He wanted desperately to have it all, but the soft rhythmic breathing coming from the beautiful woman next to him in bed said he'd have to wait to get her verdict on that idea.

He'd only just begun to drift off to sleep himself, any idea of food long forgotten now they were both sated, when his phone buzzed somewhere against the floorboards. It took him a while to locate his trousers in the dark and answer the call with a lowered voice for fear of waking Mollie and breaking the spell that they were the only people in the world tonight.

'Hello?' He scooped up his clothes and tiptoed out of the room to take the call out of earshot. It was the house landline and there was no doubt in his head that he was going to have to go home tonight after all.

'Ben? Your grandfather's behaving a little…peculiarly. I think you should come back.'

'I'm on my way.' He should be used to these calls

by now, whether emergency or false alarm, but to-night especially it felt particularly unfair. There was a lot for him and Mollie to talk over and another crisis wasn't going to help his cause to persuade her they should think about getting serious. With a heavy heart he dressed quickly and scribbled an apology note on the chalkboard shopping list hung on the kitchen wall. He'd phone her as soon as he could and beg for her forgiveness in person once he'd got this latest problem under control.

'I thought you were staying the night.' Mollie appeared in the living room wearing the sheet from her bed as an improvised toga.

'So did I.' He sighed and pulled on his shoes before this beautiful vision in white could lure him back to paradise.

'Hugh?'

'It's probably nothing major but I should go back and check he's okay.' Whatever was happening at home, he knew there was little chance of coming back here. The moment was over and probably the idea of them having a relationship beyond the bedroom.

'Of course.'

'Do you want to come with me?' He knew it was a lot to ask but he needed some sign that the next time he made his declaration of love, when she was conscious, she might reciprocate the sentiment. There couldn't be more proof of love than someone willing to go out into the cold night on another mission of mercy.

'I...er... I'm not dressed.' She made no attempt to move and all his hopes were dashed that they'd moved past what had happened that morning at his. She'd already shown her eagerness to escape the responsibility placed upon her by her own family by moving out here and he should have known taking on more was never going to end well.

'Okay. No problem.' He snatched up his keys and headed off on his own, wondering what this meant for their relationship if she didn't want to be part of his life where it mattered.

'Ben! Wait!' He looked back in time to see Mollie running across the car park after him, struggling to get arms in the sleeves of her sweater so she could button up her jeans.

'I thought you weren't coming?' The sigh of relief as she jumped into the car beside him was immense.

'I had a bit of a wobble after what happened the last time me and Hugh were in the same room together, but when it comes down to it I want to be with you, Ben. Whatever that entails.' It was the most he could expect considering everything she'd been subjected to regarding his grandfather, and he could analyse it later when he had the time. For now he was just glad he had her support.

'I'm so sorry to ruin your night but he's been behaving very oddly. Even more so than usual.' Amy rushed to meet them as they entered the apartment and ushered them towards Ben's grandfather sitting quietly in the living room.

'You were just right to call me. Grandad, how are you feeling?' There was no way of knowing from one minute to the next if he would recognise him so Ben approached with caution. He'd also asked Mollie to hang back for the time being. While he appreciated her support, he still wanted to keep her safe as well as prevent his grandfather any more distress. It reinforced the reality of the situation and what a juggling act it was going to become for all involved, but if Mollie was willing to risk it all for love then so was he.

His grandfather stared at him, unblinking.

'He'd complained of a headache earlier and feeling a bit dizzy.' Amy came to sit next to him on the settee and primped the cushions around him to make him more comfortable.

Ben had seen him confused and sometimes unco-ordinated on many occasions now, but the trouble he seemed to be having focusing on what Ben was saying suggested a new sinister element to add to his health concerns.

'Are you still dizzy? Do you have any pain anywhere?' Ben knelt beside him and waved a finger in front of his eyes to see if he could follow it. There was no initial response then, suddenly, an odd gurgling sound as his grandfather tried to form words. The right side of his mouth began to droop and the glass of water in his hand fell to the ground.

'Amy, perhaps you could go get a blanket so we can keep Hugh warm and I'll clean up the mess.' Mollie guided the only non-medical professional from the room so they could deal with what was obviously a medical emergency. His grandfather was showing all the signs of having a stroke.

'I'm going to call an ambulance, Grandad. We need to get you to hospital right away.' The loss of blood supply to the brain could be ischemic—due to a blood clot obstructing flow or haemorrhagic bleeding in or around the brain tissue—but immediate treatment was necessary as a stroke could lead to permanent disability or even death.

'I think I have some aspirin in my bag.' Mollie rifled through the pockets of her satchel bag until she found what she was looking for and popped the little white pill under Hugh's tongue. As well as a painkiller, the anti-platelet would also reduce the chances of another blood clot forming. They wouldn't know until he'd been given brain scans at the hospital if medication would be enough to dissolve any clots or he would require surgery.

The professional confidence with which she took control of proceedings gave him the space to make the emergency phone call for help without causing his grandfather any further distress. She kept his grandfather reassured and made him as comfortable as possible while they waited for the ambulance and Ben hoped this was a sign that she was on board with him come what may. Finally it seemed he had someone he could rely on.

Ben locked the door behind them as they trooped out into the entrance hall, having already dispatched Amy home with the promise to keep her up to date with his grandfather's progress.

'Are you coming with us?' he asked her as the paramedics stretchered their patient out to the ambulance.

Mollie could only watch with a growing sense of dread as they loaded the ambulance. This was a glimpse into the future if she chose to follow but her head and her feet refused to move. She loved Ben but they were yet to make a commitment to one another and here they were already in the midst of another crisis; a worrying sign of what was to come. One that could have life-changing consequences. A stroke could leave his grandfather with even greater needs than before, and as a result greater demands of those around him.

She hadn't wanted to come in the first place and get

caught up in the drama again and had only conceded when she'd seen that defeated look on Ben's face when he'd left her apartment alone. His grandfather was unpredictable and there was always that possibility of him kicking off at any given moment. She didn't want to live in the shadow of fear any more, nor of that guilt that had brought her this far.

It would only be a matter of time before the idea of love would be overtaken by a sense of duty preventing escape and she couldn't put herself in that position again. She had to get out now before it was too late. Even though her heart was breaking.

'No. This is family business, Ben.'

'Don't do this to me, Mollie. Just get in the damn ambulance.' He shouted at her, demanded she do as she was told and gave her another glimpse of that temper she was afraid was lurking, waiting until she was in too deep before it made itself truly known. Without even knowing it he'd made the decision for her.

'I'm sorry, Ben. I just can't.'

'Why are you here then? Why did you let me believe you were different…?'

The last thing she saw in that fraction of a second before they closed the ambulance doors was the haunting look of betrayal across Ben's face. She knew the timing was atrocious when he was at the lowest point already with his grandfather's health hanging in the balance, but she had to do whatever it took to protect herself. There was no one else to do it for her. Except this didn't feel any better than if they'd never slept together. If anything it was worse. She'd let them both believe they could have something more.

Mollie watched the ambulance drive away, trailing her heart along behind it and leaving nothing but shredded bloodied remains in the middle of the road. She knew his grandfather was in a bad way and naturally took precedence in Ben's thoughts. She knew it was a bad idea to tie herself down to more domestic drama after finally making her bid for independence from it. That didn't prevent her from pining for an existence with him in it.

It took every ounce of dignity and strength for her not to jump in a taxi and follow them to the hospital, but she knew this was the only way she could ever move forward in her own life.

Instead of the light sensation she expected to experience every night she returned to her quiet little flat with no one to bother her, her chest was heavy with dread on the journey home. Even now she'd made the cruellest break imaginable she couldn't help but wonder how Ben was coping or what the implications of Hugh's suspected stroke would have for them both. Or what kind of woman could do the things for them that she couldn't. She was heartbroken and alone but the tears refused to come. It wasn't going to do her any good sitting here feeling sorry for herself when it had been her choice to push away the one person she'd ever truly loved to save herself.

The Ice Queen had made her bed and now she'd have to lie in it. Alone.

Ben hoped they had enough charge in their defibrillator here for him because he was sure his heart had just stopped. He couldn't believe Mollie had done this to him again.

As they drove away, sirens blaring, the rage inside him was threatening to blow the doors out and send him running back to find her. He was angry at Mollie for not being the woman he'd imagined, but mostly he was ticked off at himself for believing he could have it all. It was unfair to ask her to take on his problems as well as her own, but he'd thought that this relationship meant more to her than either of them had admitted. He didn't know if telling her he loved her would've made things any better and now it was too late to find out. She'd made her position very clear. She valued her independence more than a relationship with him and his baggage. He pictured the dress he'd hoped to surprise her with, still hanging in his wardrobe along with all his hopes and dreams for the future. If he'd been a vindictive man he'd be planning to take a pair of scissors to it, but it was more likely he'd leave it there as a reminder never to trust a woman, or his heart, again.

He'd planned for the dance competition to be the start of something special between them, where he'd tell her how much he loved her, they'd wow the judges with their amazing chemistry and walk off into the sunset holding hands. Okay, so none of that was likely except for the part about telling her how he felt and hoping that was enough to win her heart. Now he knew it wasn't. Neither was she the woman he thought he'd fallen in love with if she could walk away so easily when he needed her most.

'Hang in there, Grandad.' He reached across the pulley and squeezed Hugh's hand but he knew they were both strong enough to get through this.

The trouble was every blow they took made the heart a little weaker.

CHAPTER TEN

THE ONLY THING more agonising than a messy break-up was the prospect of seeing the ex you loved with all your heart again. The idea of having to make small talk while all the while you could picture those intimate moments together in each other's arms was slow torture but Mollie knew she didn't have a choice. She wasn't going to leave the job she loved simply to save embarrassment and she was under no illusion Ben would either. Their jobs, their patients, depended on communication between them and as such she knew she had to tackle the problem head-on, speak to him before resentment set in and spoiled everything they'd been working towards here at the clinic.

'Can I have a few moments of your time?' She confronted him before they were due to have their first multidisciplinary meeting since she'd watched him and his grandfather leave in the ambulance. Her mouth was dry, her palms clammy, as she waited for his reaction to seeing her again.

'I think we've said all we needed to say and we both have some place to be. Unless you're thinking of ditching your responsibilities here, too?' That harsh tone was still there, making her flinch and convincing her the chances of him ever forgiving her were probably slim.

'I'm not leaving the clinic, neither are you, so I think it would be best all round if we could at least manage to be civil to each other at work.' She was doing her best to keep emotion out of her tone and let her cool alter ego handle this, but it seemed as though Frosty Knickers had thawed around the edges lately.

'Civil,' he muttered under his breath and shook his head as if she'd said something outrageously funny.

'I'm just trying to make things easier here.' Although she was beginning to wish she hadn't bothered if he was going to continue being infantile about it.

'Really? My grandfather had a stroke and you left me. How easy do you think that's been for me, Mollie?'

'I'm sorry. How is he? I heard he'd been released.' Actually, she'd gone out of her way to find out that snippet of information but it wasn't going to help this situation to admit it.

'A mild stroke. He's recovering well but, as you know, that means there's an increased risk of more in the future. You probably did the right thing in getting out when you did or you'd never have escaped that role of carer. Congratulations on your independence.' He turned his back on her to walk away and, though she deserved it, she still felt the need to justify her actions.

'That wasn't the reason I couldn't commit to you both.' She grabbed his arm tight and forced him to look at her.

'So if it wasn't his illness, what was it? Were you just looking for somebody to make yourself feel better?' Hurt oozed from every bitter word he threw at her and she hated that she'd caused him the same pain his parents and his ex had put him through. If all she could do was give him an explanation to aid the healing, she would gladly do it.

'It's the aggression I couldn't handle, Ben. I told you my father had a nasty streak and he wasn't afraid to show it, with his fists.'

'Oh, Mollie…'

'He didn't hit me but in some ways that was worse, just waiting until he would explode, watching while he beat Talia and Mum. I can't bring someone else like that back into our lives. I know it's not Hugh's fault, he doesn't know what he's doing, but I don't want to live in fear for the rest of my life.'

'I'll get him help, I swear. I'll do my best to keep him away from you. Whatever it takes we can sort it out.' There was a hope back in his voice that pierced through that wall of ice she was doing her best to re-build around her heart.

'It's not just Hugh.' She cleared her throat, preparing to pinpoint a problem that he likely didn't even know existed. 'I've seen your temper, too, remember? That time in the meeting when you shouted at me and again in the back of the ambulance. I'm simply not prepared to take the risk of ending up in the same sort of relationship as my mum. I'd rather be alone than a prisoner in my own home.'

'Seriously?' He huffed out a breath, his eyes staring at her with incredulity. 'That one time I raised my voice to you at work was after a long night with Hugh getting up every five minutes for a walkabout. I was tired and frustrated and I took it out on you. I apologise. As for being angry at you leaving me? Of course I was. I bloody loved you, Mollie, and you broke my heart. Maybe you're hyperaware of people's moods and intentions because of everything you've been through, but I am not a violent man. If you're determined not to see that then I guess there's not a lot I can do about it.

The Ice Queen reigns supreme.' He strode away as if he couldn't even bear to be in the same building as her and left Mollie wondering if she would ever see him again.

The truth did hurt. He loved her and she'd thrown it all away because she was still afraid of the past and the ghost of her father.

Mollie's pulse was beating in time to the salsa beat marking the certain success of the couple currently shimmying on the dance floor who were all smiles, sequins and snake hips and looked as though they'd both been bred in some stage-school laboratory. If they hadn't had professional training she was still a virgin, and that stirring passion every time she looked across at Ben in his tux proved that wasn't true.

It was one thing having a naïve crush on someone, but something altogether different when you were in love with a man whose body and mind you knew every inch of and that was exactly why she wanted to win him back. She'd had time to think about what he'd said and everything that had happened and she could see she'd been projecting her issues with her father onto him. Okay, so Ben had lost his cool on a couple of occasions but he was only human. Even she'd had moments when she'd acted without thinking and come to regret it. Such as the evening when Hugh had taken ill and she'd refused to get in the waiting ambulance.

She knew Ben. Deep down, past her fears and insecurities, she knew in her heart he would never do anything to hurt anybody. He was the only man she could ever picture being with and she'd let him go without taking that chance of finding out if he was 'the one.' This was supposed to be her time of living dangerously, being free, no longer trapped in that cage of fear.

She'd stuffed up but he'd still turned up for the competition and that left her with hope he would forgive her for how she'd behaved.

'Nine.'

'Nine.'

'Ten.'

The judges held up their paddles announcing the scores for the golden couple who should've quick-stepped away with the tacky glittery trophy right now and saved her from going through with this farce. There was no way she and Ben had a hope in hell of following that display and managing to come away with a grain of respect from the assembled audience. Not when they hadn't had a rehearsal together since Hugh's stroke. There was no way they could deliver a polished performance with the little time they'd had together to choreograph a routine. At this point in time she'd settle for making it through until the end of the song without completely blanking. Or breaking down. It was difficult being in the arms of the man you loved when you were no longer granted access to his life at any other time.

Their chemistry did not have to be faked for the sake of convincing spectators of their synchronicity. She was going to have more trouble pretending she wasn't madly in love with her partner and that this wasn't real.

Although the hotel venue chosen for the event held mostly colleagues and friends, the spotlight and the noise of the expectant crowd made her heart hammer as though she were about to step onto the world's stage. Not only was she going to have to find the strength to get through being pressed so close to Ben without being able to react, she was wearing her scars in public for the first time.

The dancers hadn't been required to purchase the

expensive gowns normally required for formal competition, after all this was for charity, and Mollie had planned only to wear one of her own high-neck, tattoo-and scar-covering vintage dresses, which would probably be more suitable for the lindy-hop than a waltz. When the dress he'd bought for her had arrived by special delivery with a note that simply said 'For Mollie,' she'd been overwhelmed with love and regret.

At first she'd hoped it was a sign of reconciliation and he was giving her a second chance to redeem herself. Sending a gift like that would have to prompt a woman into getting into contact but he'd rebuffed all her efforts to get in touch and refused her calls. She'd eventually had to accept there were no lines to read between, he'd probably already bought the dress long before they'd split and there was nothing else he could do with it than gift it to her. She would wear the dress, they would do the dance, earn the funding for The Shed and after that he was done with her. In the end she'd been forced to zip the dress back into its protective cover and hang it out of sight until the night of the competition before it became waterlogged with her tears and unfit for purpose.

It was a stunning aqua-blue chiffon, split up the leg and with a plunging backline which would otherwise have made her very self-conscious had so much thought not gone into the choice. The embroidered pink cherry-blossom detail simply looked like an extension of the branches tattooed on her leg and from a distance probably looked as though she'd opted for body paint rather than a spray tan. The crystal pendant backdrop from the neck hung plumb against her spine and, more importantly, followed the line of her scars. While neither of these things hid those parts of her body she wasn't particularly comfortable with, it showed he'd somehow found a beauty in those flaws she'd struggled to accept.

'Relax. You look beautiful.' Ben's voice caressed the back of her neck but the warmth of his understanding of her fears was soon replaced with the chill of reality making her shiver. This moment marked not only everything they'd worked for but also the end of their time together.

'I think the dress has a lot to do with that. Thank you.' She could feel her voice cracking from the sheer unfairness of it all and hoped he'd put it down to last-minute nerves.

'I can tell them we've had to pull out of the competition if you don't want to do this. I'll understand.' Of course he would. That was what he did best. Better than she did and sometimes to his own detriment.

'We've come all this way it would be a shame to let people down now.' As much as she wasn't looking forward to stepping out there with all eyes on her, she wanted one last memory with him to cling to and keep her company at night in her empty flat. Most of all because she didn't want to let herself down by giving into fear again when she'd come so far. The greatest shame for her would be that she was taking that next step forward in her life without him.

'No pressure, but Grandad has been looking forward to this all week.' Ben nodded out towards the crowd, and the dapper Hugh in his suit was easy to pick out in the front row seated next to Amy.

'How has he been?' Just as Ben had known she'd be fretting about her scars, she knew he'd be worrying about his grandfather the whole time he was on that dance floor.

'It gave him more of a fright than anything. Symptoms went within a matter of hours, thankfully. This time.' Ben's tone warned her he wouldn't forget how she'd reacted in his time of crisis by walking away. Even though that move had come too late to save her from getting emotionally attached to either of them.

'I'm sorry I wasn't there when you needed me. I panicked.'

'It's probably for the best. We're only at the start of this journey with dementia and there's no point in getting involved if you're not in it for the long haul. It's cool. We don't have to see each other after tonight, except at the hospital.'

'We could have so much more than that, Ben.' They did have until she'd let fear stand in the way of her potential happiness again.

'I thought we did until you ran out on us.' That sudden edge was sharp enough to cut Mollie to the bone.

'Please welcome couple number six to the dance floor, Mr Ben Sheridan and his partner Miss Mollie Forrester.' The compère announced their moment of reckoning and the cheering crowd ushering them out on the floor ensured there was no backing out now.

Ben took her hand and led her out onto the floor, both plastering on those fake smiles to hide the tumultuous emotions going on behind the scenes. She hadn't realised up until now just how much performance was involved as well as technical ability. They were going to have to act their shiny shoes off to convince the audience this was an effortless, graceful romance and not the dying act of love.

The second the music started and she was back in Ben's arms she knew there was nowhere else she wanted to be. A one-bedroom flat might have the peace and quiet she'd believed she was searching for, but this was where she truly felt at home.

She'd spotted the proud faces of her family in the audience as they'd made their graceful entrance, heard a wolf whistle she was sure came from her sister's direction, but was able to block out all distraction when it was only Ben she could truly see. As they launched into their fairy-tale dance of elegance and poise she realised life without him would be very much like waltzing here alone—a vital part was missing to make the dance complete.

'I'm sorry I wasn't there for you when you needed me. I love you, Ben. Can we try and work this out?' she whispered into his ear, not caring if this was the time or the place; she needed to finally say what was in her heart before the music stopped and everything came to an end.

She saw the set of his jaw even before he began his defensive rejection. 'I thought you didn't trust me or my temper?'

He spun her around so quickly she was light-headed, her thoughts unable to keep up with her feet.

A dip, another fake smile flashed at the judges and a moment for her brain to stop spinning before she was able to confront him again. 'Surely you can understand why I was so anxious?'

'I've already gone through this with Penny. I'm not doing it again.' He pulled her tighter to his chest as he registered the pain of past betrayal through gritted teeth.

'And I thought we'd established I'm not Penny. I want to be with you whatever it entails.'

'Love me, love my grandfather, right?' The snort of derision he gave disputed any discernible difference between Mollie and the woman who'd clearly never thought about anyone other than herself. To someone who'd gauged her purpose in life by other people's happiness, it was a devastating blow capable of making her stumble and, though Ben was strong enough to keep her in hold and on her feet, it would cost them points they could ill afford to lose. Not that a prize in a competition she'd never had in her sights counted as any significant loss next to that of the love of her life casting her aside because of her own folly.

She needed to convince him she was in this for the long haul and she was willing to be his partner in all walks of life.

Mollie broke hold and took a step back, bringing Ben to a stop along with her although the band played on over the loud speakers. She curtsied in gratitude for his time and attention as though she were a lady at court taking her leave from the gentleman on her dance card and walked away towards the audience.

With all the courage she could muster, she left the lonely figure in the spotlight and wound her way through the seats to reach her target. Hopefully that haunting image of him as she abandoned him would soon be replaced with a much happier one once he understood her motive.

'Would you care to have this dance, sir?' She held out her hand to Hugh, who raised it to his mouth and gently kissed it.

'I'd be delighted.' He rose from his chair to another round of rapturous applause and escorted her back to the floor. They crossed paths with Ben, who took his last-minute replacement with good grace, clapping as they passed and sitting out the rest of the dance in the now empty seat beside Amy. The next few minutes would likely dictate whether or not he believed she had enough love in her heart for both of them to bypass any future worries. Even without the promise of marriage she would be there—in sickness and in health.

For one heart-stopping moment he believed he'd finally driven her away for ever, his heartbreak public for all to see. These last days without her hadn't been easy and not only because of the extra care he'd had to take with his grandfather. He missed having her to share his day, his bed, and even those dance rehearsals, which had started off as a chore and ended up the highlight of his day. He'd told himself he had to protect himself from letting her get close enough again because he couldn't take another hit, but he'd never felt as vulnerable as he had when she'd left him dancing up there on his own.

That stark reminder of facing the world on his own, letting Mollie walk out of it, would have been enough for him to chase her down and beg for a second chance after all even if she hadn't veered towards his grandfather. His despair turned to awe watching her invite his grandfather up to dance with her. There was no visible sign of discomfort on her part as she approached him, no embarrassment about interrupting their performance in front of the crowd, only a genuine affection to have him involved and probably to dispel Ben's stubborn belief that she couldn't love him enough to stick around.

His grandfather was the only man he'd happily concede this dance to although it meant he'd have to wait a tad longer to attempt to salvage a future with Mollie. The joy on his face as he was transported back to his younger days tripping the light fantastic was there for everyone to see and it was all down to Mollie. She'd managed to change some of their darkest days to the brightest and Ben had almost let her go in a vain effort to protect himself from getting hurt.

She'd asked for a second chance, he wanted to be with her and tonight she'd shown true compassion for his grandfather. The only thing stopping them from being together now was his fragile heart.

As the dance ended to a rapturous standing ovation, Mollie and his grandfather took a bow and made their way back towards him.

'I hope you didn't mind too much. I thought Hugh might like one more turn around the dance floor.' Mollie's cheeks were flushed with exhilaration, her eyes shining brightly with confidence probably instilled by the audience's reaction.

'You looked wonderful out there. Both of you.' He slapped his grandfather on the back but his eyes didn't leave Mollie, so brimming full of adrenaline and love she was completely irresistible.

'You're a lucky guy, Ben. Mollie is one in a million.' There were tears in his grandfather's eyes as he shook Ben's hand, kissed Mollie on the cheek, before returning to his seat, clearly appreciative of what she'd done for him out there. As was Ben. There weren't many who would've been willing to do that unless through a sense of duty or pretence, but he knew Mollie well enough to understand the fondness she had for his grandad and the realisation of what this honour would mean to him.

'Ten.'

'Ten.'

'Ten.'

The judges got to their feet proclaiming their decision on the unusual performance. In the personal significance of the moment that element of the evening's events seemed to have been forgotten by both him and Mollie.

Her eyes widened as the crowd roared their approval of the judgement. 'That means we won!'

She grabbed Ben and Hugh both by the hands and led them back for the prize-giving ceremony, the odd trio accepting the trophy as a win for as much as family values as entertainment and commitment.

Mollie picked up the glittery prize from the plinth hurriedly set up in the middle of the floor and handed it directly to Ben's grandfather, who was standing taller and prouder than he'd seen him in a very long time, his sense of self and the achievement stronger than ever.

Ben didn't think twice about kissing Mollie full on the lips in a public display of affection, which took them both by surprise by the initial resistance he felt, soon followed by hungry acceptance. If this didn't convince her he was serious by making this commitment to their relationship as clear as she had, nothing would. This dysfunctional family was his for keeps if only he could manage to convince Mollie their shine could last longer than that of a plastic trophy after all.

Mollie had little time to contemplate the enormity of what had just happened as they were launched into a frenzy of press shots and congratulatory friends and family after the award ceremony, both she and Ben more absorbed in managing Hugh's welfare during the ensuing melee than analysing the latest development in their relationship. She was more blown away by that unexpected kiss rather than becoming the hospital's first dance champion. It wasn't simply an act of impulse. Ben would never have made such a move without considering the consequences for even a split second and the impact it would have on their working relationship as well as their personal one. Even the tight grip he had on her waist as they posed for celebratory photos announced his possession to the assembled crowd and that was exactly what he'd done. He'd taken ownership of her heart, body and soul even if he hadn't truly believed it until tonight.

She waited until the furore had died down and a happy, but exhausted, Hugh had gone home with Amy to add the latest trophy to his cabinet of treasures before she demanded clarification from Ben about the recent developments.

'So, Mr Sheridan, did that kiss happen merely in the heat of the moment or…?' She helped herself to a glass at the champagne reception laid on for the participants following their win.

The music had ended; there was no reason for them to keep on dancing unless Ben had decided she was worth putting in the time and commitment. She gulped down some liquid courage for the moment of reckoning, but the bubbles rushing across her tongue and down her throat so quickly made her choke before she could finish the most important question she could ever remember having to ask. The one that should've ended with a 'do you actually love me?' base from which she could either build on this relationship or raze it to the ground once and for all.

He took her glass from her, set it back down onto the table, grabbed her hand and pulled her away from the throng of well-wishers who'd barely given them a second to themselves. Even as they tried to make their way over to the side of the room they had to delay their need for privacy in the wake of well-meaning handshakes and hearty congratulations en route.

Inside she was screaming at people to move so she could end the misery of not knowing if she'd done enough to convince her man she was genuine about wanting to be with him. Outwardly, however, she'd perfected that strained smile and polite facade because up until recently other people's feelings had always been more important than her own. Except in her haste to reclaim control of her life she'd neglected to realise something more important than a need for space—love—and now it might be too late to get it back.

To her surprise he kept on walking until the thinning crowd was far behind them, through the doors to the lobby and out onto the patio outside. Under the white arbour and the blush of the climbing pink roses where many a romantic proposal had probably taken place, Ben finally turned to face her. Mollie held her breath until those familiar blue eyes locked and reminded her she had nothing to fear. He had that way of looking at her that made her feel as though they were the only two people on the planet to help her work through her worries.

He cupped his hand to the back of her head and dipped down to capture her mouth with his in a passionate kiss that reminded her to breathe so she could keep doing this without dying from a lack of oxygen. Every kiss felt like the first, and the best.

'Does this feel as though it's only happening in the heat of the moment?'

It took a few seconds for Mollie to register he'd stopped kissing her when her lips were still tingling from his touch. 'I...er... No... Maybe we should do it again just so I can be sure.'

She leaned in until his smile touched her lips and he performed an encore every bit as good as the original performance.

'This is for me and you, no one else. Not for Grandad, Amy, Talia or anyone else. Dancing or no dancing, I want to be with you, Mollie. I love you. Everything else, well—'

'We'll work it out.' They were a team, and a winning one at that. They'd proved that time and again.

EPILOGUE

BEN TOOK A deep breath before he reached for the door. Mollie squeezed his hand. 'It'll be fine.'

She understood the worry about coming here when every time was different. They never knew who exactly they were going to encounter on the other side of that door. Sometimes Hugh was his lovely self, happy to see them both and on occasion even go out for a spot of lunch in the country. On the bad days, though, he could be bad-tempered and unpredictable and confused about what they were doing there. Which made delivering news like this all the more daunting when his reaction might be far from the one they wanted.

'Hey, Grandad.' Ben walked in first, greeting him with a broad smile and a hug as he did every time even when he didn't know what response he would solicit from his greeting.

'Ben! Mollie! How lovely to see you.' Hugh rose from his seat immediately and kissed them both on the cheek.

Mollie could feel the relief emanating from Ben as his grandad welcomed the visit. Today was a good day.

'How are you keeping, Hugh?' She gave him a hug, then set about unpacking the treats they had brought him from home, including his favourite chocolate biscuits and a blanket Amy had crocheted for him. Although they didn't see as much of her as they used to they still kept in touch and she was always keen to hear news on Hugh.

'Fine. I can't complain. There was a lovely lad came yesterday and cut my hair for me. I like to look my best, you know.' He ran his hand over his freshly cropped hair and Mollie noticed he'd had a shave too and looked more like his old self. It was easier for Ben to see him like this so he didn't feel as guilty about having to move him into the care home. Not that he had any reason to think he'd done anything but his best for his grandfather. It had simply become too much for them all to handle after the second stroke. He needed twenty-four-hour care and this was the only place they could be certain he was safe. Thankfully it seemed to be working out and the home wasn't too far from the apartment so they were free to visit any time.

'We have some news, Grandad.' Ben got straight to the point and Mollie knew he couldn't contain the excitement. They'd agreed not to tell anyone else until he'd had the chance to break the news to his grandfather first even though he was bursting to shout it from the rooftops.

'Mollie's pregnant.' Hugh stole his thunder and left them both open-mouthed.

'How did you know?'

'I'm a doctor, Ben, not an idiot. I can see the glow in both of you a mile away.'

Mollie burst out laughing. So much for the big secret. It probably was spread a mile wide over their faces when the pregnancy had come as such a happy surprise to both of them even though she'd apparently been pregnant throughout the break-up and the dance competition without even knowing it. Perhaps she could even blame her initial lapse of judgement over their relationship on the hormones.

They hadn't reached the stage of discussing a family but now things were settling down for all of them she knew it would all work out. Especially when Talia was nearing her due date, too. They could embark on motherhood together, bringing them all closer together than ever.

'Well, we might manage one more surprise.' Mollie handed the ultrasound photograph to Ben so he could have his moment of glory.

It took a moment for Hugh to register what they were showing him and Mollie thought for a second they might have to spell it out for him. Then he did a double take and stared at them both with that same look of wonder Ben had when the sonographer had pointed out there were two heartbeats on the screen.

'Twins?'

'Yup.' The proud daddy was already puffing out his chest so much there was a danger he might actually combust with pride when his babies were born.

'So are you going to get married or what?' Blunt as ever, Hugh had Ben rolling his eyes at the comment.

'For goodness' sake, Grandad. Can you let me do this properly, please?' He dropped to one knee, which in the cramped bedroom was no mean feat.

'What are you doing?' The significance of the gesture didn't hit Mollie until he took out a small velvet box from his pocket and opened it to reveal a stunning diamond ring.

'Mollie Forrester, my dance partner, the love of my life and now mother of my babies, will you marry me?'

Tears sprang to her eyes. 'Yes, of course. I love you, Ben.'

As he placed the ring on her finger images appeared in her head of her future as Mrs Sheridan with family all around her and a lifetime together. She couldn't have been happier.

* * * * *

MILLS & BOON

Coming next month

ONE NIGHT WITH DR NIKOLAIDES
Annie O'Neil

"Cailey *mou*. I've always felt we had a connection, you and I. Don't you know that?"

She shook her head against his finger, fighting the urge to open her lips and draw it into her mouth. Any connection they'd had had been more master and servant than anything. She'd grown up working in his house. Scrubbing, cooking and cleaning alongside her mother, who had spent her entire adult life serving as the Nikolaides housekeeper.

She'd thought that kiss they'd shared all those years ago had been a dare. A cruel one at that. For it had been only a day later when she'd overheard him telling his friends he'd never marry a housemaid.

She was surprised to see him looking hurt. Genuinely hurt.

"Not in the strictest sense," she whispered against his finger.

"We're peas in a pod. You must know that. And today, working together, wasn't that proof?"

"No. It only proves we work well together. Our lives… we're so different."

She wanted to hear him say it. Say he'd held himself apart from her because of her background.

"You *are* different from me," he said, lowering his head until his lips whispered against hers. "You're better."

Before she could craft a single lucid thought they were kissing. Softly at first. Not tentatively, as a pair of teenagers might have approached their first kiss, more as if each touch, each moment they were sharing, spoke to the fact that they had belonged together all along.

Simply kissing him was an erotic pleasure on its own. The short walk to Theo's house had given his lips a slight tang of the sea. Emboldened by his sure touch, Cailey swept her tongue along Theo's lower lip, a trill of excitement following in the wake of his moan of approbation.

The kisses grew in strength and depth. Theo pulled her closer to him, his lips parting to taste and explore her mouth. The hunger and fatigue they'd felt on leaving the clinic were swept into the dark shadows as light and energy grew within each of them like a living force of its own.

Undiluted sexual attraction flared hot and bright within her, the flames licking at her belly, her breasts, her inner thighs, as if it had been waiting for exactly this moment to present itself. Molten, age-old, pent-up, magically realized and released desire.

Continue reading
ONE NIGHT WITH DR NIKOLAIDES
Annie O'Neil

Available next month
www.millsandboon.co.uk

LET'S TALK
Romance

For exclusive extracts, competitions
and special offers, find us online: